# What the Neighborhood Knows

## A Psychological Domestic Thriller with Several Twists

### Kristina Fox

Kristina Fox

ISBN (paperback): 979-8-9931619-3-8

ISBN (eBook): 979-8-9931619-4-5

To Rich—my favorite alibi.

# Contents

Keith's house
Seamus & Darby's house
Mrs. Nelson & Molly's house
Gemma's house
Victoria & Emilio's house
Welcome to Sycamore Way
Brooks & Ali's house
Fiona's house
Freddy & Penelope's house

# Prologue

SHE SMILES AS SHE stabs me one last time—the type of smile you practice in the mirror. Polished, patient, perfect. There was no rage in her eyes, no trembling of her hand. The heavy silence of satisfaction lingers in the air. She planned this. I can tell. I try to speak, but blood rises instead of words. She leans closer, not to comfort me, but to watch. To make sure the job is done. I catch the scent of her vanilla shampoo on her long brown hair as it sweeps past my nose. I should have seen it coming. I taught her how to lie, how to hide the bruises, and wear silence like armor. I broke her down piece by piece. And now, she's giving me back what's left.

# Chapter 1

Victoria

We pull into the driveway of 251 Sycamore Way. I'm surprised the old, weathered Chevy he purchased as a mechanic's special made it. The houses here are small, but each has its own character, with lush lawns and gardens that burst with color. Unlike the cookie-cutter tract homes and endless condos of the big city we left behind, this neighborhood is alive and unique. He cuts the ignition, which silences both the engine and the song I'd been bouncing along to—ironically, *Our Lips Are Sealed* by the Go-Go's—before turning to look at me.

"We're here," Emilio says. His green eyes sparkled with excitement.

The cheerful blue house smiles down at me. This is it...home. Arms wrapped around my belly, a little smile of gratitude peeked at the corners of my mouth. A rush of emotion washes over me, and a rogue tear rolls down my cheek. I wipe it away.

"This is the start of our new life. Be happy," he says.

Emilio circles around to the passenger side of the car to open my door and give me his hand. I sweep my long black hair behind me, then grasp his hand. My thighs are sweaty from the drive, and I fix my dress so I don't give the neighbors a show. Emilio lifts our bags out of the trunk, humming as he does so.

"Should we check out the house before we unpack?"

Emilio laughs. "We only have two bags each. It's not like there's a chest of drawers in here."

He's right. The butterflies in my stomach flutter about. I'm excited and nervous about our new beginning. I take a deep breath of fresh suburban air and say, "Well, little one. We made it." The slight kick in my belly confirms my words.

As we enter the house, the scent of floor polish envelops us. It's reminiscent of my grandparents' house. The hardwood floors creak as I make my way from the foyer into the front room. The shabby-chic decor gives the house a cozy atmosphere. Although it's only one thousand square feet, it feels like a mansion compared to my one-bedroom apartment back home.

"Hun?" Emilio calls me from upstairs. I cringe. I've never liked terms of endearment.

"Yes?" I answered.

"Come up and take a look at this."

The second floor reveals two bedrooms and one bathroom. Emilio's tall, lean body is illuminated in the doorway of the bedroom. I follow his gaze and cover my mouth with my hand to hide my surprise. A surge of emotions rises as I choke back tears. The room is painted soft blue with fluffy white clouds on one wall. In the far corner sits a white crib, an airplane mobile floating over it.

"How did...?"

"I told the realtor you're pregnant with a baby boy. It looks like she thought making this room into a nursery would make us happy. It's okay, right?" Emilio asks. He turns to face me.

"It's better than okay," I say, walking over to the white dresser. I touched its shiny lacquer. In the top drawer lies a small Bible. There's an inscription on the first page.

"This Bible belongs to: my sweet boy. May God always be with you," I read out loud.

I turn to face Emilio, but he has moved on to the master bedroom. I put the Bible back and headed in his direction. Emilio plops down on the bed and pats the space next to him.

"Hey, no shoes on the bed," I tell him as I swat at his feet.

"You're too serious," Emilio says. "Don't worry. You can relax now."

He's right. I'm so uptight. I peek into the bathroom and jump at the sound of the doorbell. Emilio laughs.

"Here, sit down. I'll get it," he says.

Instead, I follow Emilio downstairs. The silhouette of a woman appears on our front porch, and my breath catches. Who could it be? No one knows we're here except the realtor. I grabbed Emilio's arm to stop him from opening the door.

"Don't worry," he whispers. "It'll be fine."

A woman with medium-length, light brown, wavy hair stands on our porch, a large basket in her arms. Her friendly smile and demeanor fit the cheerful suburban energy the neighborhood emanates.

"Hi there! You must be the Carusos," the woman says. "I'm Gemma, your next-door neighbor. I wanted to stop by and introduce myself and welcome you to the neighborhood. Here's a little something for you both."

Judging by the way Emilio winces as he accepts the basket, it must be heavy.

"This is so generous. Thank you. I'm Emilio, and this is my wife, Victoria," Emilio says. "Excuse me while I put this down."

I smile shyly at Gemma and say, "It's nice to meet you. How long have you lived here?"

"Oh, I've lived in Laurelville all my life. Born and raised. But I've lived on Sycamore for about ten years. I live over there in that little house with my German Shepherd, Chester."

I nod and peek over at the single-story, eggshell-colored house next door. Encircled by a cute white picket fence, a flurry of sunflowers lines the bay window, and a curvy cobblestone path runs from the front gate to her stoop.

"You'll love living here," she continues. "We're having our annual Fourth of July picnic next week. It's a Sycamore Way tradition. There will be plenty of food, and the forecast is sunshine."

"Fourth of July picnic?" Emilio asks. A heavy foreboding looms in the pit of my stomach. The plan was to move here and lie low. A neighborhood picnic is not in the plan.

# Chapter 2

Victoria

As Emilio makes dinner, I pace back and forth and brainstorm ways to get out of the Fourth of July picnic. Finally, Emilio guides me over to the kitchen table and sits me down. He warms a mug of hot water in the microwave and places a tea bag in it.

"Where did you find tea?" I ask him.

"In the drawer," he answers. "Here, blow on it and drink. Your anxiety can't be okay for the baby," Emilio says.

I sigh and do as he says.

"You're right. But we agreed that we wouldn't draw attention to ourselves, at least at the start. A Fourth of July picnic is not laying low, Emilio. Who knows who will be there?"

"Honey, it is not a citywide rager. It is a potluck block party with plenty of delicious dishes to share. Although we want to lay low, we also need to fit in here so that we don't seem suspicious or odd in any way. If it makes you feel better, we can arrive late and leave early."

Again, I cringe at the word "honey" even though I need to play the role of a loving wife. Emilio and I have discussed this. I say we don't have to pretend when we're the only ones in the room. He says if we don't play our roles, it'll be easier for one of us to slip up. I see what he's saying, but using terms of endearment is annoying and unnatural to me. In any case, I brush away my irritation. "Promise?"

"I promise."

Emilio sets down a plate of fettuccine Alfredo in front of me. It has little chunks of chicken or tuna in it.

"Wow, where did you get the food to cook?" I ask as I twirl the pasta around the fork tines. "Is this chicken or tuna?"

"It's chicken. There are packages of pasta and jarred sauces in the cupboard, along with cans of chicken *and* tuna. The owner of the property told me she had stocked some staples for us. You'll like the owner. Tomorrow, we can make a trip to the store."

I take a bite and close my eyes as the warm pasta soothes my palate. The creamy meal is what I need to relax.

"Mm, why does this meal taste like the best meal I've had in forever?" I ask. My nerves began to calm.

"Because it's the closest thing we've had to homemade in two months," he answers.

***

After dinner, I sit on the Victorian-print sofa as Emilio unties the ribbon on Gemma's gift basket. The purple satin ribbon slides off to display an assortment of goodies. I lift out a bottle of Taittinger champagne and set it on the coffee table.

"For after the baby is born," I say, patting the bottle.

Next up is a collection of mason jars filled with baked goods, each one labeled by hand. The jars contain macarons, biscotti, and mini versions of chocolate chip cookies, snickerdoodles, and vanilla scones. Emilio unscrews the lid to the jar of biscotti and takes a cookie out. He *is* Italian, after all. Biscotti are baked twice, so they should be hard enough to allow for dipping in coffee or tea. Emilio takes a bite.

"Wow," he says. "These are perfect. A hint of cinnamon. They remind me of my aunt's biscotti. Gemma gets a ten out of ten for these."

Emilio hands me the other half of his biscotti to try, but I decline.

"No thanks," I say as I enjoy a macaron. The macaron is perfect with its crunchy outer shell and delicious raspberry filling.

"Yep! Ten out of ten for her macarons, too."

"We'll get fat living here if we keep this up," Emilio laughs, then reaches for another item in the basket. "What's this?"

It's a laminated card with a Post-it note stuck to it. The note reads: "Hi, here is a list of a few of the popular places in town."

I take the card from Emilio and read it aloud.

"It lists restaurants organized by type of food, fun activities, grocery stores, coffee shops, beauty shops, and even bookstores.

Apparently, this small town has quite a bit to offer. I wonder if any of them deliver."

"I'm sure they deliver. We still live in America," Emilio says jokingly.

I set the card aside and lift a candle out of the basket. The label says, "Welcome to the Neighborhood." The scent of warm vanilla and cinnamon fills my nostrils as I inhale. It smells heavenly.

The last item is a light-blue velvet bag. *What could this be?* I give it a gentle squeeze. Pulling the mouth of the bag open, I peer inside and find a fluffy white polar bear and footy pajamas with a little polar bear stitched on the front. The tag reads: 3-6 months.

"This is so sweet. So, does everyone on the block know about the little guy? And here I thought we would sneak in and mind our own business," I say, a little worried that we made the wrong move.

"It's a small town, Hun. I'm sure word gets around about everything," Emilio replies as he rubs my shoulders. Although I'm not a fan of being touched, my body has been so achy in recent days, and the massage is welcome. Over the past two months, my swollen ankles and backaches have become more painful.

"All you need to do is make small talk and smile," he says. "Everything will be fine."

# Chapter 3

Gemma

On my way back home, my neighbor and best friend, Ali, pulls up in her black BMW SUV. Ali and I have known one another since she and her husband, Brooks, moved to Sycamore Way six years ago, when their daughter, Sydney, was a newborn. Ali pulls up to the curb and rolls her window down. She removes her oversized Chanel sunglasses. Her strawberry-blonde hair is in a messy bun atop her head. It looks like she went through a wind machine. Sydney is in the backseat playing a game on her tablet and looks up as the car comes to a stop.

"Hey guys, what are you up to?" I ask.

"Hi Auntie Gemma! We went to McDonald's because Mommy said it's too late to cook and she's tired," Sydney says, holding up her Happy Meal. "I got a Hello Kitty toy."

"Mother of the year. I know," Ali says, her words dripping with sarcasm. "In my defense, I was at the animal shelter all day. We had three adoptions—two dogs and one cat."

"That's fantastic, Ali! I love when animals find their forever home," I say. Well, that accounts for the messy hair. Ali gets right down on the floor and plays with those animals as if they were her own.

"Were you out for a walk?" Ali asks.

"No, I delivered a welcome basket to our new neighbors," I say as I glance toward the Caruso's house.

"What are they like?" Ali whispers.

"Sweet. Quiet. I think the guy might be Spanish or Italian. He's tall and on the thin side. And the woman is about our age, Caucasian, and has long, black hair. Victoria and Emilio."

"Didn't you mention that she's pregnant, too?"

"Yes. I'd say she's maybe seven or eight months along. I invited them to the Fourth of July picnic next week, so everyone on the block will get to meet them."

Ali snickers.

"Huh? What was that for?" I ask.

"I was imagining what her first impression of Seamus will be," she says, covering her mouth to stifle her giggles.

I laugh too. Seamus is the flirt on the block. A large, buff Irishman with fire-engine red hair, he often makes inappropriate jokes and comments to the ladies on the block, especially when he's had a few too many drinks. The only one who has ever called him on it was Brooks, Ali's husband. Since then, Seamus has toned it down a bit. He's still moderately offensive, though. We all put up with it for his girlfriend's sake. Darby is a sweet, bohemian creature who is in a world of her own. You can tell from the way she dotes on Seamus that she loves him with every ounce of her being. Whether or not she realizes that he's such a brute is questionable. They have an adorable four-year-old daughter named Ramona.

"Maybe one of us should warn her," I say.

"I'll leave that up to you," Ali says. "You're better at breaking in the new people than I am."

I rolled my eyes at her. "Gee, thanks."

"I'd better get this little one inside," she says, tilting her head toward Sydney. "You want to come over for a glass of wine later and hang out? Brooks is out of town this week, so it's only Syd and me until Saturday."

"Sure! Text me once you've got the Syd-meister all settled in."

Sydney laughs at my nickname for her. I blow her a kiss, and she blows one back.

"Auntie Gemma, you're so funny," she says as Ali drives away.

I open my front door and am greeted by my six-year-old German Shepherd, Chester. His coat is still shiny from the bath the groomers gave him yesterday.

"Hey, buddy. How ya doing?" I say as I scratch the top of his head. Chester's tail wags wildly and follows me into the kitchen.

Scraps of cellophane and ribbon litter my kitchen table. I toss them into the bin and put away the excess crafting materials and tools. It's 6:30 p.m., so I make myself a quick bite to eat before heading over to Ali's.

I mash and season half an avocado and toast a slice of sourdough. As I stare out the kitchen window, I am reminded that I have a clear view into the Carusos' kitchen. The house was vacant for most of the time I've lived here. There's an energy about that house that has always given me strange vibes. I'm glad Emilio and Victoria are bringing new life into it. Maybe all the lonely old house needed was a nice family to occupy it.

After devouring my toast, I take Chester out for a walk around the block. As the sun makes a slow exit, lights throughout the neighborhood flicker on. We arrive back home, and Chester laps at his water bowl. He lies down, content and relaxed. My phone dings. It's a text from Ali telling me to come over when I'm ready. I grab a light sweater and head out. As I wander down my driveway, shivers travel down my back even though the air is warm and still. I peek over to the Caruso's house. The lights are off, but as my eyes refocus, I think I see a shadow in the window on the top floor. I wave, but as quickly as the shadow appeared, it vanishes. That's odd. I do a double-take. There's no one there. I must have been imagining it.

# Chapter 4

Victoria

My white T-shirt and blue boxer shorts wrap around me as I toss and turn. My belly protrudes between them, and I can't get comfortable. Emilio is snoring, and his lips form a little smile. After staying in off-the-grid motels for the past two months, I know he's relieved to be in a place we can call home. I am too. My anxiety is difficult to push aside, though. It nags at me constantly.

Careful not to wake Emilio, I scoot myself out of bed and shuffle down to the kitchen. I peek in the drawers and cupboards and find pasta, sauces, and various canned goods. The kitchen's wood cabinetry is beautifully finished in a reddish-brown stain; the countertops have a cream and grey marbled pattern. A drawer reveals several boxes of tea and instant coffee envelopes, along with a handful of restaurant-style sugar packets. The cupboards contain plates, glasses, and mugs. The large black mug that reads "Love's Travel Stop" on the front with a little red heart is the perfect size. Emilio and I passed several Love's locations as we made our way to Laurelville. Perusing the selection of teas, I decide on vanilla chamomile. This will soothe my anxiety.

While waiting for my tea to steep, I pull out my phone and flip it open. Then, I remember it's not a smartphone. I can't access Instagram, Facebook, or even my email. The only person who has this number is Emilio. It's pretty much useless except in case of an emergency, so I set the phone back on the kitchen counter.

Standing at the living room window, I sway back and forth and caress my belly. A small pile of leaves dances across the front lawn. The neighborhood is dark except for one bright light in the window of a house down the street. Maybe someone else has insomnia.

From the corner of my eye, I catch movement. A shadow of a person? I step away from the window, and the sudden motion makes me spill a bit of my tea. What's out there? Maybe it's more leaves. Or perhaps a stray cat. *You've got to get a hold of yourself, Victoria. Stop being such a scaredy-cat. You're fine. You're safe. Emilio made sure of all of that.*

"Victoria?" I hear Emilio call my name from upstairs. A little part of me is annoyed because I was enjoying the quiet time alone, and yet I know Emilio is here to protect me.

"Down here," I say.

"Are you okay?" he says, rushing down the stairs.

I turn around to face him.

"Yes. I'm fine. I couldn't sleep," I say with an edge in my voice that I immediately regret. Emilio has been so good to me.

"Little guy keeping you up?" he asks.

"That and we're in a new place. I'll get used to it."

# Chapter 5

VICTORIA

The rich aroma of freshly brewed coffee wakes me from a deep slumber. My eyes ease open, and for a moment I'm unfamiliar with my surroundings. My arms embrace my baby as I stand and take a deep breath. We're home. I look over to Emilio's side of the bed, which is neatly smoothed over.

"Good morning, sunshine," Emilio greets me. Sitting on the kitchen counter are two to-go cups, two white pastry bags, and a small container of fresh fruit. A shift in my belly almost makes me lose my balance. The baby must be hungry, too.

"The coffee shop down the street had these. I hope they're okay," Emilio says before I can ask where the goodies came from. He slides the contents of the pastry bags onto small plates to reveal egg and bacon bagels, a scent that makes me ravenous.

"Wow, this looks so good. Thank you," I say, as I take a huge bite. The food warms my belly on contact, and my shoulders relax as I savor each bite.

Emilio kisses me on the top of my head.

"You and the baby need to eat and stay strong," he says. "Carbs and lots of protein for energy and strength."

I take a sip of coffee, expecting it to be black with a splash of almond milk, my go-to, but it's not coffee. It's a delicious half-caff soy vanilla latte. The edges of my mouth curl up into a huge grin, which makes Emilio burst with pride.

"I did good, right?"

"Mm, hmm! This is such a treat. I haven't had a vanilla latte in..." I think back to the last time I had a real coffee.

"Two months," he says. "I don't know about you, but I'm sick of gas station and motel coffee. I thought we deserved something special."

"Well, this is the perfect start to our new lives. Thank you, Emilio," I say.

Emilio pulls out the little green notebook and tiny pencil he uses to make lists. He flips the notebook open and says, "Okay, so first on the list for today is grocery shopping. Then, I'll see where I can find a job. We're in a good place right now, money-wise, so I'm not too worried. It helped that we prepaid for a year of rent."

Emilio and I planned this move and went over each detail multiple times. He did most of the work. It was Emilio who found the house, worked with the realtor, and budgeted how much we would need for the two months in transit to Laurelville and for the first few months of our lives here. My job was to squirrel away as much money as I could and tie up loose ends, such as canceling credit cards and securing the money from the trust my grandparents left me. The cash I withdrew from each paycheck added up. As a nurse in a large hospital, I took home a decent salary. The extra shifts I picked up here and there helped. Emilio's job as a mechanic had brought in a decent salary as well.

After breakfast, Emilio and I prepare to start our day. I pull two one-hundred-dollar bills from my stash, which I have hidden in different places, and slide them into my wallet. I inspect my photo ID.

"Victoria Caruso," I whisper to myself. No more Cara Livingston. She doesn't exist anymore. I am Victoria Caruso. I repeat my new name several more times, as if it's a mantra.

"Ready?" Emilio says, his voice startling me. "Sorry, I didn't mean to scare you."

"I'm ready," I answer.

Emilio peeks out the window before he opens the front door. I follow his gaze to the purple house across the street from Gemma's. There is a silver Mercedes parked in front.

"Is there something wrong?" I ask him.

"No, you can never be too careful. Even though we're in a safe place, be sure to always stay alert."

An ominous feeling appears in my gut.

"Do you think he's found us?" I ask, a hitch in my voice.

Emilio turns to me. "No, no. I'm sure it's nothing."

"Emilio, tell me."

"Everything's fine."

I shoot him a skeptical look.

"Okay, okay. When I came downstairs earlier, the corner of the rug was flipped up. I don't remember it like that last night, do you?"

I think back to the night before and shake my head.

"Do you think...?" I start to ask.

Emilio interrupts me. "I'm sure it's nothing. Do you have your phone?"

"I'll grab it," I tell him. I remember I left it on the kitchen counter the night before.

The phone isn't there, though. I scan the counter and search the living room. Where did it go?

"Emilio? Did you move my phone?"

"No. I believe it was on the counter last night before we went back to bed."

"It's not here," I say, as I squat down to check the floor, beneath the table, and behind the small appliances. "Where could it have gone?"

"Did you use it to call someone?" he asks.

I roll my eyes at him. Of course, I wouldn't have used the phone to call anyone. The burner is for Emilio and me to communicate with one another in case we get separated. I never used the phone, so it should still have all its original minutes.

"Here, let me call it with my phone," he says.

Emilio calls the number, and we wait for my phone to ring. Silence.

"You had the ringer on, right?"

"Yes, it was on," I say, a knot in my throat. "You don't think..."

"I'm sure it's somewhere around here. We'll find it. Don't worry."

I nod. I'm sure I left it on the counter last night, though. *Where did the phone disappear to? Did someone break in to steal my phone and accidentally flip the corner of the rug? Who would do that?* My stomach does a flip-flop, and I'm not sure if it's the baby or my unrelenting anxiety.

***

The town is so small that it takes us less than three minutes to drive to the grocery store. It would be easy for me to walk here with the baby once he's born. As we walk down the aisles, I stay close to Emilio, the thought of someone in our house unnerving. We pick up necessities—meat, cheese, butter. I spot a jar of locally made cherry preserves, my favorite. Emilio adds a few bottles of wine to the cart.

As we make our way toward the produce section, I see Gemma, who appears deep in thought. She's holding two avocados in the air. She doesn't see us at first, and I almost don't say hello because she is very clearly having a conversation with the fruit.

"Umm, hi. Gemma?" I say.

She comes to life like one of those plastic dolls with the blinking eyes. She reminds me a little of the good witch Glinda in The Wizard of Oz, but with darker hair.

"Victoria! And Emilio! Hello! It's so wonderful to see you out and about. How was your first night in the house?" she asks.

"It was fine. The house is wonderful," I say, trying not to let my fear shine through. "Thank you so much for the treats in the basket. It was so thoughtful of you. Emilio said your biscotti is some of the best he's ever tasted. And he's Italian, so that's a huge compliment."

Gemma smiles. "Indeed, it is. I, too, have Italian roots."

Emilio perks up and asks, "What part of Italy is your family from?"

"My family is from Florence," she answers.

"Mine is from Livorno," Emilio responds.

Gemma smiles, "What a coincidence. Our families are practically neighbors."

"It is no wonder your biscotti are so perfect," Emilio says with a warm smile.

"I make a mean ragù as well. You two will have to come over for dinner soon. Do you both like spicy foods?" Gemma asks.

"We do," Emilio says. "Although Victoria has been experiencing some heartburn. I told her it will probably go away once the baby is born."

"Did your mother ever give you Brioschi when you were little?" Gemma asks Emilio.

Emilio feigns surprise as he says, "You know about Brioschi? My aunt used to give that to me when I had an upset stomach. I forgot all about it until now. Victoria, honey, we'll have to get some for you. It's a lemony baking soda drink that cures heartburn and other stomach ailments. It tastes awful, but it works."

"I have a container at home," Gemma says. "I'll drop it by later today."

"I will try anything," I say. I try to maintain a cheerful demeanor when, in fact, I feel the urgent need to get out of here. *Why does Emilio have to be so damn friendly?*

"Oh, before I forget. What can we contribute to the picnic?" Emilio asks.

"Well, I'll be curating the main dishes. This year, it will be a Mediterranean theme. Ali is bringing a huge Greek salad, Darby baklava, and I believe Fiona said she would bring a Mediterranean veggie platter with olives, cucumbers, carrots, and bell peppers. I told her I would mix up a large batch of hummus to complement the platter," Gemma pauses. "How about beverages? Sparkling and still waters?"

"And wine!" Emilio says.

"Yes, wine would be wonderful. Ali said she would also make a batch of whiskey sours. I know it doesn't go with the Mediterranean theme, but her husband, Brooks, is a huge whiskey fan."

"It all sounds wonderful," I say, although I can hear the anxiety in my voice. "I can't wait to meet everyone."

"You two will fit right in," Gemma says. "You'll have a blast."

Emilio and I say goodbye and promise to stop by later for the Italian antacid stuff. Emilio rubs me on the back of my shoulder and says, "I'm so proud of you. You're getting the hang of it. Gemma's nice. There is nothing to worry about. Her family is from Florence. Our families are practically neighbors."

"Okay, Mr. I-want-to-be-friends-with-everyone. Maybe you're right. I'll give it a chance. But it still doesn't explain my phone's disappearance."

"I'll go pick us up actual phones this week. How about that?" Emilio asks.

I perk up. That's the best news I've heard in two months.

"Promise?" I ask.

"I promise. We'll need to remain anonymous online, though. We can create new social media accounts, but ones that are faceless," Emilio says. "And no contacting old friends."

"What about Scarlett?" I say. I ask even though I know what his answer will be. Scarlett is my best friend, whom I have known since we were four years old. It kills me that I can't talk to her every day. Although one night from an old motel in the desert, I gave in and called her at work from a payphone. I wanted to let her know I was okay. I could tell it broke her heart that she couldn't call or help me. The no-Scarlett rule may be the one rule of Emilio's I have to override. I hope it's not the one that gets me killed.

# Chapter 6



VICTORIA

Emilio keeps his eyes on the road, the afternoon sunlight slanting through the windshield and casting long golden streaks across the dashboard. The weather in Laurelville is warm, and I roll my window down to catch a breath of the clean summer air.

"We've got one more stop before home," he says calmly and matter-of-factly. "Are you okay?"

I tilt my head back against the seat. The trees blur by. A slight, weary whine escapes my lips. I pull down my T-shirt, which has risen from shifting positions so much. My clothes don't fit well lately. My slender frame has morphed into a body that is so foreign to me. I've grown curves that never existed before. My breasts and butt are embarrassingly huge, and I complain about them all the time. Emilio tells me I look beautiful, but I certainly don't feel it. Although my clothes are too small, it makes little sense for me to buy new ones. I'm only a couple of months away from delivering. Uncomfortable and cranky, I try not to take it out on Emilio. My hormones are out of control.

"Do we really have to?" I ask, the words are more whiny than inquisitive.

The car hums steadily beneath us, but I absorb every bump in the pavement as though it's magnified. Pregnancy has turned even the simplest errands into marathons, and right now, the thought of one more stop makes me want to curl up and surrender to sleep.

"Where are we going?" I ask him.

"I want you to meet someone. You like our new house, right?"

"Of course. It's amazing, Emilio. I know I don't say it all the time, but I appreciate everything you've done for me. And the baby."

"And you like the baby's room?" he asks me.

"I love it. It was unexpected, but a very welcome surprise. It was very thoughtful of the owners," I tell him.

A group of office buildings and a fitness center come into view as Emilio pulls into a large lot. Through the fitness center windows, I see people on treadmills and bikes huffing and puffing.

He leads me into the building. The sign on the door reads "Heritage Realty." Now I get it.

A lonely, empty chair sits behind a wooden desk smattered with dust-covered file folders. The brown tweed carpet has seen better days. A long hallway with several closed doors spans the length of the building. Emilio taps the little bell on the desk, and a woman in her sixties with dark hair streaked with rich burgundy highlights emerges. She greets us with a warm smile.

"Emilio, hello," the woman says. "And you must be Victoria. You have perfect timing. I just got here myself."

The woman holds her hand, clad with several gold rings, out, and I lean forward to shake it.

"Honey, this is Fiona. She's the realtor who rented us the house. I don't know if I mentioned this, but Fiona also owns the house," Emilio explains to me.

I'm at a loss for words. No wonder the house is so immaculate. Fiona is the owner *and* realtor. *Why didn't Emilio mention that before?*

"I...I don't know what to say," I stutter. "Thank you so much. The house is perfect. I love it."

"You're welcome," she replies. "I hope you enjoy it. The house has been vacant for a few years. When the last tenant moved out, I took my time remodeling it from top to bottom, so practically everything in it is brand new. Some of the furniture is vintage. When Emilio told me about you and your family, I knew the house would be the perfect fit."

"My family?" I say, confused. *Why would Emilio tell her about my mom and dad? Or Jack?*

Fiona peeks at my belly, and I realize the family she is referring to is me, Emilio, and the baby. I feel stupid for thinking Emilio told her about my past. Of course, he didn't.

"Oh, yes, well, once the baby is here, I guess that is what we will be. A family. Our family," I say awkwardly, although I may have made myself look like more of an idiot. I guess I could always blame it on pregnancy brain.

"I almost forgot," Emilio says, revealing a bottle of red wine we purchased at the store. "This is for you. It's not much. A small token of our appreciation."

Fiona takes the bottle and reads the label.

"Amarone. How did you know? It's one of my favorites. Thank you, dear," Fiona says, and places it down on the desk.

I'm thinking about what to say next when I remember what Gemma said at the market.

"Are you the same Fiona coming to the Fourth of July picnic on Sycamore? I think Gemma said something about a veggie platter?" I ask, then second-guess myself. "Or maybe I have the name wrong."

"Yes, I am *that* Fiona. I live in the purple house on Sycamore, three doors down from the corner," she says, then sighs and shakes her head. "Gemma and her damn Fourth of July picnic. We have it every year. It's almost sacrilegious not to attend. What did she sucker you two into bringing?"

"She gave us something easy, beverages. But I'll make an Italian dessert as well," Emilio says.

"Everyone likes a delicious dessert," Fiona says. She smiles at Emilio, and I notice a glimmer in her eye. *Is she flirting with him?*

"We'd better get home. We have ice cream in the car," Emilio says.

We say goodbye to Fiona, and she retreats down the hallway. Before leaving, I notice the caddy of business cards on the front desk and take the one that reads "Fiona Adams, Realtor." Her number may come in handy.

"What do you think?" Emilio asks as we walk back to the car. "Perfect situation, right?"

"Umm, sure," I say, even though I got an odd vibe from Fiona, "Isn't it a little strange that she owns the house we live in, and she lives on the same street?"

"Why is that strange? I feel a very motherly vibe from Fiona. Her guidance is what gave us this house in this community."

"You're right. And I trust you. I'm sure if she were creepy, you would have picked up on it by now. But do you think she watches us? To make sure we're not doing anything wrong?"

"Like what? Accidentally kill a plant? Overwater the lawn? You're so paranoid."

I guess he's right. Meeting new people makes me uneasy. I'm sure everything will be fine. So far, the neighbors seem nice enough.

***

When we finally get home, I feel like I don't have a single ounce of energy left. I sink into the couch, eliciting instant back pain relief. I shut my eyes for a minute, take a few deep breaths, and allow myself to enjoy the comfortable position for a few minutes before standing to help Emilio with the groceries.

"No, no. You sit back down. I'll unpack the groceries. Why don't you kick your shoes off and put your feet up? Those ankles are not happy," Emilio tells me.

I peer down at my feet and ankles. Eww. They're red, puffy, and swollen. Disgusting. I remove my shoes and plop back down on the couch and place a pillow under my feet.

"Uh, Victoria?" Emilio calls from the kitchen.

"Yes?"

My gaze follows his to a spot on the kitchen counter. It's my burner phone. At that moment, the phone buzzes. Emilio rushes over to it, and I watch the color drain from his face.

"What? Who is it?" I ask him.

It takes a minute as he opens the flip phone. His eyes dart back and forth.

"Emilio, what is it?" I ask impatiently.

"It's a message from Fiona. I forgot, I gave her our numbers when I signed the lease for the house."

He hands me the phone, and I see a pixelated text message that reads, "So fantastic to meet you both today. Enjoy the house."

"It still doesn't explain why the phone went missing," I tell him. "Or how it returned."

# Chapter 7



Over the next few days, we settle into the house, gathering what we need for the months ahead. From groceries to baby supplies, there's always something to purchase. My belly grows larger by the day, and the baby's movements are faster and stronger. The Fourth of July arrives before we know it. We've already been here for a week and a half.

The cases of sparkling Pellegrino and still water for the picnic are stacked by the front door. Emilio assembles a tiramisu for the picnic, and after a meticulous final dusting of cocoa, he places it in our insulated cooler. I take a deep breath, and Emilio frowns.

"It will be fine. Relax," he says.

Emilio wheels the dolly of beverages out the front door, and I follow closely behind with the dessert. Orange cones and "Caution: children at play" signs sit at both ends of the street. The sound of children laughing and playing echoes through the air. Two side-by-side picnic tables with umbrellas sit in the middle of Sycamore Way. Gemma is busy arranging plates and bowls, as a woman with long, strawberry-blonde hair and delicate features assists her. The spread is immaculate, and I curiously scan each dish.

"Victoria! Emilio! You're here," Gemma says as I hand her the cooler. "This is my friend Ali. Ali, meet Victoria and Emilio. They moved into the blue house at the end of the block."

Ali smiles and says, "Hi, welcome to the neighborhood. I live in the house to the right of Fiona's with my husband, Brooks, and daughter Sydney. The annual Fourth of July Sycamore Way picnic is always a big hit. Gemma makes giant portions, so make sure you eat up."

Gemma laughs and replies, "I love to feed people. It's my love language."

"That's an understatement," Ali says.

Gemma peers into the cooler I gave her and removes the tiramisu.

"This looks authentic. Did you fly to Italy and back to pick it up?" she jokes.

"Emilio made it this morning. It's his specialty," I reply.

The sound of little feet approaches, and a small girl with long blonde hair appears, giggling. She grabs Ali's leg as a boy about the same age with brown hair and an American flag T-shirt appears. He taps her on the shoulder and laughs.

"Tag! You're it, Sydney!" he says.

She replies with, "Okay, okay. Time out for a minute. I want to get a drink. It's hot out here. Where did the others go?"

Gemma hands the girl and boy each a kid-size water from a large cooler.

"I dunno. I think Oakley and Ramona went to help Ramona's mom," the boy says.

Ali turns to me and says, "This is my daughter, Sydney. She's six going on sixteen. And this is Brodie. His parents are Freddy and Penelope. They live in the yellow house across from you and Gemma."

"Well, hello there," I say to the two children who smile, wave, and then run off to play.

"What I would do for a fraction of that energy," Ali says, chuckling.

There is a short bout of silence as Gemma and Ali rearrange a few more items on the table. The spread could easily feed a hundred people. I eye the falafel and hummus.

"What can I do to help?" I ask.

"I think we're all set," Gemma replies as a woman in her forties arrives pushing an elderly lady in a wheelchair. "Oh, Molly and Mrs. Nelson. I'm so happy you made it. I'd like you to meet our new neighbor, Victoria."

Gemma explains that Molly has been Mrs. Nelson's nurse for the past two years. I smile politely as Molly hands Gemma a box of store-bought cookies. Although Mrs. Nelson is getting up there in age, I can tell by the sparkle in her eyes that she is very alert and aware of her surroundings. She seems to enjoy the chitter chatter of her neighbors and the laughter of the children as they play.

"Mrs. Nelson has lived here on Sycamore for longer than I have," Gemma says.

"That's right, Gemma dear," Mrs. Nelson says. "I remember the day you moved in. I've been here thirty-two years now. We moved in three years after my dear husband, Ronald, God rest his soul, closed his practice and said, 'Hey Ginny, we're moving to Laurelville.'"

"What kind of practice did your husband have?" I ask.

"He was an obstetrician/gynecologist. Believe it or not, he delivered Molly, right here. He sure loved seeing those little babies thrive. Kept in touch with a handful of them throughout the years. I'm so lucky that Molly was available to care for me after he passed."

"Ron passed about two months before I came to Laurelville," Molly tells me. "I wish I had moved here earlier so I could have had some time with him. I was working at a hospital in Nevada that was severely understaffed. My boss pulled a lot of strings for me to leave and come help Ginny."

Molly gently rests her hand on Mrs. Nelson's shoulder. Mrs. Nelson places her hand on top of Molly's and looks up at her with a warm smile. "I sure am glad you're here."

"Oh, here come the others. Let me introduce you," Gemma says to me, then turns to Molly and Mrs. Nelson. "You two enjoy yourself. There's plenty of food. Ginny, I think Ali brought some whiskey sours. I know how you love those."

Ginny winks at Gemma, and she and Molly head over to the food. A robust man with red hair and a petite woman with blonde braids with a streak of pink in them are headed our direction. The woman is carrying a platter of baklava. My mouth waters at the smell of honey and butter. A little girl with short blonde hair runs to catch up with the couple.

"Victoria, this is Seamus, Darby, and Ramona. They live in the pink house with the flowers painted on the side over there," Gemma tells me. "Darby is an artist and a healer. Ramona is four."

Seamus devours me with his eyes, and I get chills. "Well, aren't you a beauty?" he says. He takes my hand in his oversized ones and kisses it. He gives me the heebie-jeebies, and I quickly pull my hand back. His grin reminds me of the Cheshire Cat in Alice in Wonderland.

"Uh, thanks," I say. Gemma mentioned something about one neighbor being a bit *pervy*. She said he was harmless. That might be true, but he sure is creepy.

Darby says, "Oh, don't mind him. Seamus is a very sexual creature. You'll get used to him."

This comment makes the coffee in my belly want to come up. I'm pretty sure that I won't get used to Seamus. As I try to forget that Darby said his name and the word "sexual" in the same sentence, she leans in and gives me a bear hug. I catch a whiff of lemongrass and patchouli. My first instinct is to back away. I've never been an affectionate person. And hugging a stranger is out of the question. Neither my mother nor my father expressed love through touch.

My mother was a fully functioning alcoholic who enjoyed her martinis. My father was an abusive misogynist. His abuse was both physical and emotional, and I believe this is what caused my mother to turn to alcohol. He never laid a hand on me, but often I would wake up to my mother's cries and my father's shouting. She attempted to cover up her blooming bruises and black eyes with makeup, but I knew better. I could never understand why she wouldn't take me and leave him. As a young child, I spent a lot of time at my grandparents' house. Then, when I was fourteen, my mother passed away from liver disease. By then, both sets of grandparents had passed away. My father's parents had left me a sizable trust. However, I could not access the money until I was thirty years old. I ran away from my abusive father and went to live with my best friend Scarlett, the one person I'm indebted to for life. She was my salvation. Scarlett hid me in her room, and I lived with her for almost five years. Her parents never knew. Scarlett and I were lucky all those years that we never got caught. Although I think her mom may have known. While in high school, I earned extra money from babysitting and odd jobs around town. When I turned eighteen, I was hired at the local diner and saved enough money to rent a tiny room in a rundown house shared by five other people. Although I had been dealt a losing hand in life, I never gave up. Plus, I was smart. I put myself through nursing school and was hired at the local hospital. The hospital was where I met my future husband, Jack.

# Chapter 8



I run home to retrieve a large bag of to-go containers. Everyone loves the food. My neighbors ask me what I used in each dish and compliment the flavor combinations. Despite this, there is still plenty left on the table. Even Fiona takes a hefty helping of chicken shawarma, pita, hummus, and Greek salad to go.

"Gemma, I have to say, you outdid yourself this year. The food is delicious. You know I'm not one for leftovers, but I could eat this Mediterranean fare every day of the week. It's so fresh. And the flavors. Fantastic," she says, giving me a chef's kiss as she takes a pita triangle, dips it in the tzatziki, and places it into her mouth.

Fiona is a bit of an odd duck. Some people think she gives off that vibe of being standoffish. Still, once you get to know her, she's quite entertaining, especially after a few glasses of wine. A few times, she has joined in on the neighborhood girls' nights. The last time Fiona spent time with us, she told us some juicy Laurelville gossip about one realtor in her office who shacked up with the mayor. The girls had a field day with that one, since both the realtor and the mayor are married.

"No!" Penelope said. "I know his wife. She's so hip and cool. And they have three kids. There's no way he's cheating on her."

"They were caught red-handed by one of my realtors in the office. The information is rock solid," Fiona said with a sly look on her face.

"How did he, or she, catch them?" I asked. "And the mayor? He's like more than sixty years old. How old is the realtor he's having an affair with?"

"She's thirty-five. And hey, I'm sixty." Fiona laughed. "You know sixty is the new forty. They were caught in the lot of the Travel 8 Motel down the road. The donut shop is next door, and the realtor who saw them had promised her kids she would grab a dozen. When she saw the mayor and the realtor together, she told me immediately," Fiona said, her hands animated as she explained the scenario.

Penelope was the nosy one in the group. She loved gossip.

"So, what were they doing?" Penelope asked. "We need details."

Ali rolled her eyes. "No, we do not need details. Penelope, you have two children. Use your imagination. Two adults, motel. We do not need the visual.

Darby nodded in agreement. The wine and gossip continued to flow, and the conversation floated from one topic to the next.

I'm brought back into the present when a little hand taps my leg.

"Auntie Gemma, did you make your yummy flag cookies this year?" Sydney asks me, a little dollop of hummus on the side of her mouth.

I take a napkin and laugh. I wipe the hummus off her mouth.

"Oh, thank you for reminding me, Sydney. I almost forgot. They're on my kitchen counter. Could you do me a favor and ask your mom to pass these out while I go in and get them?" I ask. I set the bag of takeout containers in front of her.

"Sure, Auntie Gemma," Sydney says. She skips over to Ali, who is chatting with Darby and Seamus.

As I head home, I see Victoria and Emilio by themselves at the end of the table. Emilio is rubbing Victoria's shoulder. I hope they aren't uncomfortable around our neighbors. I take this as my cue to step in.

"Victoria, could you help me with something?" I ask. "And Emilio, did you know that Freddy over there is Italian as well? He was born in Parma."

"Parma is a beautiful city," Emilio says. He takes the cue and heads over to where Freddy and Brooks are.

Victoria is quiet as she follows me to my house.

"I know it can be a bit overwhelming to meet so many new people at once," I tell her. I sense she's a bit anxious.

"Oh, no. Everyone is so nice. Nowadays, I run out of steam very quickly. This little guy has me up all hours of the night already," Victoria says as she rubs her belly.

"When is your due date?" I ask, handing her a small plate of Italian anisette cookies to carry out to the table. I pick up the larger tray of my famous American flag cookies, and we head back out.

"September fifth," she says. "About two more months to go. I'm ready, though."

I nod. "Have you decided on a name yet?"

"I've narrowed the list down to two names, Luca and Sebastian," she says.

"Two strong Italian names. I love it," I say, and she lights up at my comment. "You know, if you or Emilio ever need anything, please don't hesitate to ask. I'm right next door, and I work from home."

"You're very sweet. Thank you," she says with a warm smile. "What do you do for work?"

"I'm a children's book author and illustrator. I also volunteer at the local library a few days a month," I tell her.

The little cinnamon-colored specks in her brown eyes sparkle in the warm Southern California sun as her face lights up.

"That's wonderful. I would love to see some of your work. Books were my best friend as a child. I plan on reading a lot to this little one," she says as she pats her belly.

I nod. "How about I send you the link to my author page so you can choose the ones you like? I have several stray copies lying around the house. I'll bring them over."

"I would love that. Yes, please send me the link," she says. She places the plate of cookies down on the table, and I do the same with the large tray. "How many books have you published?"

"So far, the count is up to thirty-two. I'm working on a series about a black kitten and a green worm who are best friends."

"That sounds adorable," she says. "I'm sure you're very talented. Did you always want to be a children's author?"

I'm about to answer when Victoria whips her head around to look at the entrance of Sycamore Way. I look and don't see anything, but hear the noise of a loud muffler backfire.

"Are you okay?" I ask her.

The color in Victoria's face changes from a healthy glow to the whiteness of a sheet of paper. She opens her mouth to answer, but nothing comes out. I grab her hand as she gasps for air.

"Emilio!" I call out as Victoria crumbles to the ground in front of me, my arms straining to cushion her fall.

# Chapter 9



Victoria

A familiar beeping stirs in my head, but I can't quite pinpoint what it is. My eyelids are as heavy as boulders as I attempt to open them, disoriented. I take a breath but immediately cough from the acrid scent of disinfectant, urine, and some other nasty odor. *What happened?* My first thought goes to my baby and if he's okay. I reach for my belly, hoping for some sign of movement. A tear rolls down my cheek. *Why am I here?* I remember Gemma and the plate of cookies. The machine beeps louder and faster as my heart rate rises in panic. I squeeze the bedrail and close my eyes. I take a few deep breaths. The beeping falls into a slower rhythm.

"Victoria!"

Emilio rushes into the room with a small Styrofoam cup.

"You're awake. Here, let me get the nurse."

He sets the cup down on the side table and runs back out of the room.

"Mrs. Caruso, you gave us quite a scare there. How are you feeling?" the nurse says as she checks my vitals, her stethoscope cold to the touch.

"A little woozy," I say, moving my hand to touch the back of my head. "What happened? Is my baby okay?"

The nurse grabs my hand and says, "Oh, don't touch there. The doctor gave you two stitches but left them uncovered so he wouldn't have to shave your head to place a bandage. It's still healing, so be very careful. The fall gave you a concussion and that cut on the back of your head, but luckily, one of your neighbors caught you and softened the blow. Your husband and neighbors acted quickly, and the paramedics arrived in record time. Your baby is fine. Active little fella. We did an ultrasound while you were sleeping, and his heartbeat is strong."

"Oh, thank God. Thank you so much," I say, as a deep sense of relief flows through my body.

"Of course. Now, you rest, okay? You're not in the clear yet. We want to keep you here for a few days under observation."

"But I..." I start to protest, but Emilio cuts me off.

"Victoria, you need to rest. It's not the time to argue. You of all people should know better."

I know what he means and smile at the nurse. That used to be me in purple scrubs, helping sick people. It's funny how being on the patient side of things is so foreign to me.

The nurse leaves to get the doctor so that he can perform more tests. Emilio sips his coffee as he holds my hand.

He whispers to me. "Do you remember what happened?"

I close my eyes and try to recall what happened at the picnic. Gemma. The cookies. Gemma's children's books. Then I remember. I thought I had spotted a blue Subaru BRZ at the opening of our street. The same car that Jack drives. But Jack is miles away. There's no way he found us. *Is there?*

The thought of Jack finding us makes me nauseous. My heart rate rises again. Sweat beads on my brow. The room spins. Faster. Faster. I close my eyes. I can't breathe. *Why can't I breathe?*

"Nurse! Nurse! Please help!" I hear Emilio's voice in the distance. It's like he's a million miles away.

# Chapter 10

VICTORIA

The doctor ran tests galore to make sure the baby and I were okay. My dizziness was a result of a concussion or brain bruise. Once the swelling went down, the dizziness stopped. I'm thankful Emilio purchased health insurance for us before we arrived in Laurelville. I can't imagine how much an out-of-pocket four-day hospital stay would cost.

During my stay at Laurelville General Hospital, you would have thought I was the most popular girl in town. Although we arrived on Sycamore Way a little over a week ago, several neighbors came to visit.

Of course, Gemma visited the most. She made something called penicillin soup, a hearty chicken soup that she claimed was a miracle healer. She also delivered delicious stews and pastas to help me build strength. Her beef bourguignon was out of this world. I made a mental note to get her a thank-you gift once I'm fully well. I thanked her and apologized profusely for fainting into her arms that day at the picnic.

"Don't be silly," she said. "Why are you sorry? I'm the one who should be sorry."

"You? Gemma, why would you be sorry?"

"I'm sorry my reaction time wasn't better. Before I knew it, you were on the ground, and your head was bleeding," she said.

"The doctor said you softened the blow. The cut on my head would have been a lot worse if it weren't for you," I told her, and I reached for her hand to convince her.

"Well, I'm glad you're okay," she said.

Ali and Sydney came by with some homemade sugar cookies and beef bone broth. Both hit the spot. Sydney was very excited about the baby and asked if she could babysit one day.

"Maybe once you're a little older. I think that's a wonderful idea, though. In the meantime, you can help me with him."

"Oh, Mama, can I? Can I help Auntie Victoria with the baby? Please? Pretty please?"

Ali laughed and mouthed, "Sorry" to me. I didn't know what to do or say, so I smiled at her. It surprised me a little when Sydney called me auntie, but I guess at that age, a lot of kids call women they know auntie even if they aren't related.

"Well, only if she says it's alright. No pestering her, or me, about it, okay?" Ali said to Sydney. "If Victoria needs help, she'll tell you."

"Okay, Mama. I'll be the best helper," Sydney said, her bright green eyes lit up in excitement.

Seamus and Darby showed up with a colorful knit neck pillow and an embroidered fleece eye mask. Darby crafted both items by hand, and I became overwhelmed with gratitude. It must have been the hormones because I am a very unemotional person. I was embarrassed when my eyes welled up. Of course, Darby gave me a gentle hug and rubbed my back. I was surprised to find her touch so calming.

"I feel so stupid crying," I laughed. The beautifully fashioned items had exceptional quality. It was as if I could feel they were made with love. "This might be the nicest thing anyone has ever given me."

I realized after I said it what my remark implied and said, "Not that I don't love all the food and goodies everyone has brought me. After this debacle, I think the neighbors of Sycamore Way deserve an award for their hospitality."

I continued to blabber on as Darby rubbed my back. Seamus gave a hearty laugh. Darby nudged him. I stopped mid-sentence. *Did I miss something funny?*

"Ignore him," Darby said.

"She's a witch," Seamus blurted.

"Shut up. I am not a witch. It's not my fault that you don't understand what it means to be a healer," Darby said. A deep wrinkle formed in her brow.

"I'm...I'm confused. What is he talking about?" I asked.

"I'll tell you what. When you get out of the hospital, the ladies of Sycamore will have a girls' night. I'll explain my healing practice to you then. In the meantime, use the pillow and mask and get some rest. They're both infused with lavender and chamomile, so they should relax you," Darby said with a gentle smile.

As she and Seamus left, I heard her down the hall.

"I'm so through with you, Seamus. I am not a witch. Essential oils and candles do not equal witchcraft. You got it?"

Seamus mumbled something inaudible after that. I don't know why, but it made me laugh—a big guy scolded by a small Bohemian woman. I admit Darby is one feisty lady.

Even Fiona visited with a bag of freshly baked croissants and a container of tomato bisque. She entered the room with an air of authority and gave me a small smile and a gentle pat on the shoulder as she handed me the bag, which I opened to reveal the most wonderful buttery aroma. My stomach growled.

"Fiona, these smell amazing. You shouldn't have," I told her.

"Oh, I didn't make them myself. I'm not Gemma," she said with a chuckle. "I picked them up from the French bakery a few minutes ago, so they *are* fresh out of the oven. You make sure you feed that baby well. We want him to grow up to be as big and strong as his father."

I must have made a face because Fiona became flustered.

"Emilio is such a wonderful father figure. We want his baby to follow in his footsteps, don't we?"

I nodded and thanked her once more for the delicacies. As I sat in the hospital with nothing better to do than let my mind race, I wondered what Emilio told her about us and our situation. The way Fiona emphasized the word father made me uneasy. Of course, it could be my paranoia. I feel like I'm being watched all the time.

# Chapter 11

Gemma

Emilio and Victoria pull into their driveway a little after noon. Emilio is such a gentleman and always opens Victoria's car door to help her out. Emilio is sexy in that lean, muscular sort of way. His olive skin shows off his Italian heritage, and there's a softness in his eyes as he speaks to you.

My neck is tired from being hunched over my kitchen table/makeshift desk all day. As I finish the latest edits to my newest children's book, my stomach gives a moderate rumble. I pop some leftover pasta into the microwave, fill Chester's bowls with kibble and water, and an idea pops into my head. I'll take a little break and go to the store. I'll pick up ingredients for a meatloaf dinner to bring to the Carusos' house later. Emilio and Victoria must be exhausted with the move, the baby, and Victoria's time in the hospital. I grab a few of my books as well.

As I open the door to my black Ford Fusion, a bright blue older model F-250 with a U-Haul trailer attached arrives on our street. I send a group text to Ali and Darby.

Do you guys see the truck that pulled into the house next to Darby's?

Three dots pop up, and a text from Ali appears.

Must be the new guy.

*New guy? What new guy is she talking about?*

What new guy? Darby texts back.

Don't you remember? Fiona told us at our last girls' night that some contractor guy had rented the old Hadley house.

I guess Darby and I had too much wine that night. I don't remember that at all. I text back.

Same. Darby says with a laughing emoji and a wine glass emoji.

The text message thread goes silent as I stare to see who will step out of the truck. From my car, I can see Ali's curtain move ever so slightly, so I know she's watching too. I'm sure Darby, who has a clear view of her new next-door neighbor, is at her window as well. The truck door opens, and out steps a man. His attire comprises a baseball cap, a flannel shirt, and blue jeans. His Timberlands are worn, and although he's several houses down, I see his hands are big and strong. His build is stocky, and he's also quite tall.

My phone buzzes. It's Ali on FaceTime. I pick up, and she mouths a series of words to me.

"What? I can't hear you," I tell her.

"I said, did you see him?" Ali whispers.

"Why, yes. Yes, I did," I answer. "It looks like our block is the next Wisteria Lane."

Ali rolls her eyes. "That would make us Desperate Housewives. No thanks. He looks somewhat familiar, don't you think?"

"No, I would know if I met a guy who looked like that. And speak for yourself. I'll be the Teri Hatcher character any day."

"You can't be her. She's the one who can't cook," Ali says. "You have to be Bree."

We laugh and make plans to get together later for a chat and a glass of wine. I look. It's 1:00 p.m. The new guy has the back door of the U-Haul rolled up. He takes off his baseball cap, which reveals military-cut light brown hair. I gawk as he removes his flannel shirt. His bulging muscles and tan skin look like they've stepped out of the pages of Muscle and Fitness magazine. His white tank top also reveals a tattoo on his shoulder, although I can't quite see what the design is. As he turns and faces my direction, for a second I think he can see me, and I blush.

# Chapter 12



"So, just to be clear, you didn't tell Fiona that you aren't the baby's father?"

"Of course not, Victoria. What do you take me for? An idiot?" Emilio replies, a bit agitated at my remark.

"I'm sorry. When Fiona said we want him to grow up to be as big and strong as his father, it struck a nerve. Because, no offense, Emilio, and you are a lot of things, I don't think anyone would describe you as 'big and strong.' Even though you work out, you're more of the lean and sexy type."

Emilio smiles at the sound of my words. "So, you think I'm sexy?"

"You know what I mean. Jack would be described as big and strong. He's the stereotypical G.I. Joe. I was worried..." I trail off.

"What have I told you? As far as everyone here is concerned, we are Emilio and Victoria Caruso, a happily married couple with a baby on the way. No one needs to know that we're hiding from your soon-to-be ex-husband."

I nod. "You're right. It must be my imagination. Thinking I saw Jack on the day of the picnic, the missing cell phone, and Fiona's remark have made me over-the-top anxious."

"How about you take a warm shower and change into some comfortable clothes. I'll make us an afternoon snack. We can sit on the porch and enjoy it. The weather outside is excellent."

"How about we invite Gemma to join us? I'd like to give her the gift we bought for her. She's been so thoughtful ever since we arrived. When I was in the hospital, I did a lot of thinking. I've let my nerves get to me, and these past several months have not been easy. But, Emilio, you're right, getting to know the neighbors is the right thing to do. After all, this is home."

"Now, you're getting the hang of it. Okay, you go take care of yourself. I'll meet you on the porch," Emilio says. He gives me a quick hug in reassurance.

***

The water cascades down my back and envelops me in a warmth that soothes my body. A deep breath fills my lungs, and I relax with every exhale. My vision is blurry with my contacts out, but I wipe the water from my face and reach for the shampoo bottle. As I hum a familiar tune, I squeeze a bit of shampoo onto the top of my head and gently massage it into my hair and scalp, careful to avoid my stitches. As I rinse, there's an odd chemical-like smell in the air. I take a whiff of the soap on my hands and do a double-take as I notice clumps of straight black hair between my fingers. My stomach performs a flip-flop, and I feel sick. Why is my hair coming out? Why does my shampoo have such a sickly odor? Why didn't I notice this when I poured it out? I panic as more hair pulls loose from my scalp. I scream for Emilio, and he races up the stairs to me.

"Victoria, what's wrong?" he says from outside the shower door. I open the door. I don't care that Emilio will see my naked body. This is an emergency. I show him the clumps of hair in each hand. Tears stream down my face.

"What is happening?" he asks. "Why is your hair like that?"

I have no words. Emilio grabs a towel and wraps it around me. He leads me to the bedroom and sits me on the bed.

"There's something bad in my shampoo," I tell him.

"What could it be? Who would do that?" he asks. "No one's been in the house. I've always made sure to lock it."

"Are you sure?" I ask.

"Yes, I am very sure."

"And no one broke in?"

He shakes his head. "There's no sign of anyone being in this house but us."

"Who else has the key to the house?" I ask. But we both know the answer to that question.

"Victoria, we can't blame Fiona without proof she did it. Plus, why would she do that?" Emilio asks. "That doesn't make any sense."

"Well, she does seem to have a little crush on you. Maybe she wants to get rid of me to get to you. You need to tell her that I'm not a threat."

Emilio makes a face of disgust and says, "Don't be ridiculous. First, Fiona is old enough to be my mother. She is a very nice lady and has set us up in this amazing house. Plus, you're the one I want to be with. You know that. Why would Fiona want to hurt either of us? Second, if I told her you're not a threat, it would blow our cover. You don't want that, do you?"

I sigh and then shake my head. "I don't understand. Why can't I live a normal life? What did I do to deserve this?"

"You're a good person. Good things will come. You'll see," Emilio says. He pulls me closer to him. I feel so vulnerable right now. Emilio's soft gaze comforts me, though, and as I look him in the eye, it brings me back to the day I first met him.

***

"Hey, Babe! Go grab me a beer, will ya? Grab two. It's fuckin hot out here," Jack yells to me from the carport below our apartment.

"Coming!" I yell back over the balcony rail. I run over to the fridge and grab two bottles of Budweiser.

As I reach the carport, I see a man next to the car that Jack is now underneath.

"Oh, um, hi," I say to the man. He's around the same age as Jack and me, maybe a little younger. He's tall, and his coloring and build are the exact opposite of Jack's—tall and lanky with green eyes and olive skin. Even though Jack has green eyes, too, this guy's eyes are a darker green.

Jack rolls back out from under the car. His tan body glimmers with sweat, and the long scar that runs from his sternum to his belly button is visible. It's a reminder of the car accident that killed his parents many years ago. His dirty blond hair is long enough to get in his eye, and he shakes it off. I still think he's as sexy as the day I met him.

"Babe, this is Tony. Tony moved here from Italy, and we work at the shop together."

I hand each of them a beer and wish I had brought one down for myself.

"It's nice to meet you, Cara. Jack has told me a lot about you," Tony says. I can tell he's a gentle soul from the way he shakes my hand and puts his other hand on top.

"Same," I say.

"Hey, hey, no hitting on my girl there. I don't care what they call you. What is it? The Italian Stallion," Jack gives a hearty laugh, but his eyes say that he means business.

"Were you born in Italy?" I ask.

"No, I was born here in California, but I was raised in Livorno by my aunt. Livorno is in the Tuscany region," Tony explains.

"All I know about Tuscany is that there are gorgeous sunflowers there."

"That part is true. You would love it. Jack, you should take Cara to Italy one day."

From that day on, Tony makes a weekly appearance. Sometimes he comes over for dinner. Other times, he and Jack go out drinking. Scarlett and I tag along from time to time. As Jack and I get to know Tony, I feel like I could trust our Italian friend. I also know he has a slight crush on me. Anytime I say I like or want something, somehow it magically appears.

# Chapter 13

VICTORIA

Jack and I first crossed paths in the emergency room of San Francisco General Hospital. I was at the end of my twelve-hour shift when I saw him in the waiting room. He was pacing back and forth. He looked up at me, his green eyes wet with the threat of a tear.

"Mr. Livingston?" I asked. I attempted to maintain a professional tone. He was devilishly handsome, and I noted an automatic spark of attraction.

Jack nodded. "Yeah, that's me. You can call me Jack. How is Larry?"

"Your friend is with the surgeon right now. We'll keep you updated on his status. Does he have any family you can call?"

"No. No family. Will he be okay? Did we make it here on time?"

"It's too early to know, but Dr. Sheffield is the best in the business. If there's anyone who can save your friend, it's him."

"Thank you," Jack said, the corners of his mouth turned up slightly in appreciation. "What's your name?"

"I'm Cara."

"I'm Jack," he said. "Oh, sorry. I already said that. Okay, I'll wait here until Larry is out of surgery. The guy is newly divorced. He doesn't have anyone. The guys at the shop are the closest he has to family."

I nodded and headed back to the nurses' station, where the other two nurses on duty gave me a sly look.

"What?" I ask.

"He likes you," my friend Melanie said.

"Stop. He's worried about his friend. And rightfully so. That laceration to his stomach was very deep."

"Umm, hmm," she said, then winked at me and left to check on a patient.

A half-hour later, I glanced up at the clock. The shift change would happen soon, so I double-checked that I had completed my tasks and that the patients' charts were updated. As I finished up, I sensed someone approaching from behind. I turn and then jump.

"Sorry, I didn't mean to scare you," Jack said. "Is there any word on Larry?"

"Let me see," I said, as I moved to the other side of the desk to access the computer. "It says here they're still in surgery. Looks like it'll be a while."

Jack looked down at his watch. "Is there a place that serves breakfast around here other than the cafeteria? I'm starving."

"Yeah, Newkirk's is right around the corner," I told him. "They make a mean fried egg breakfast sandwich."

His stomach growled, and we laughed. "Any chance you'd like to join me?"

My heart pounded in my chest as his green eyes caught mine once again. I managed to pull it together to answer him.

"Uh, sure. Once I finish up here, I can leave. I should be done in two minutes. Do you want to meet me there?"

"I'll wait," he said, and pointed to the waiting room.

I finished my charts as little butterflies danced in my stomach.

"I told you," Melanie said as she bumped my shoulder.

"It's only a meal," I told her, and then tried to convince myself as well.

"Uh, huh," she said as she winked at me.

*** 

As we walked to Newkirk's, Jack asked me about myself, a welcome change from other guys I had recently met. I had gone on at least six dates in the past six months, and every guy was the same. They talked about themselves and how a job in finance was the greatest thing ever. They boasted about getting promoted into some grand, top-of-the-ladder position. I learned to accept drinks or coffee on a first date, never a full meal. Once, I even had to call Scarlett for a rescue call. I couldn't even make it through one glass of wine because the guy was so repulsive. He had smelly breath and yellow teeth and kept moving his hand closer to me to touch my leg and kiss me. So gross. Not Jack. Jack was a gentleman, and we fell into easy conversation.

I told him about my childhood and teenage years and how I put myself through nursing school. As I spoke, his bright green eyes were set on mine as if I were the only person in the room. When I asked him about his life, Jack said he enlisted in the Army at eighteen.

"So, what do you do for work?" I asked him.

"I'm a mechanic over at Superior Auto," Jack said. "My buddy in the ER is also a mechanic. He was working on the exhaust system of a car when a metal piece that wasn't secure swung down at him."

"That makes sense. The injury was very deep."

The conversation stopped for a moment. I could tell Jack was worried about his friend as he ran his hand through his dirty-blond hair.

"Enough about me," he said. "Tell me more about you. I'm impressed that you put yourself through nursing school. You must be extremely strong-willed and focused."

I laughed. No one had ever called me strong-willed before. It was more like I was trying to survive. Who knows where I would have ended up if I hadn't pushed myself?

Jack looked at me, confused. I shook my head.

"No, no, you're right. Thank you. That's a big compliment. I think focused is the right word."

"So, do you have a boyfriend?"

I looked at him, surprised by his bluntness. But I liked it. His eyes drew me in. The physical attraction was undeniable, but the energy that flew between us was indescribable. By our third date, I was one hundred percent smitten and certain this was the man that I would marry.

# Chapter 14

Gemma

I twirl over to the refrigerator, my arms in a dramatic pirouette, as Beethoven reaches a crescendo in his No. 5 symphony. I read an article about how this classical piece might reduce your risk of cancer. The factual accuracy of this information is up for debate since the study was solely performed on lab rats. Either way, classical music puts me in a lively mood. I crack a few eggs into the meatloaf ingredients as they blend in my KitchenAid stand-up mixer. I pack the mixture into my loaf pan and into the preheated oven.

As I clean my counter off, I glance out the window where I see Emilio in the Caruso's kitchen. He washes a few clusters of grapes before he looks up and sees me. I wave, and he reciprocates with a wide smile. Before I know it, there is a knock at my front door.

"Emilio! Hello! How are you and Victoria today?" I say, as I slide my dishwashing glove off.

"Hi, Gemma. We're well. I put together a tray of cheese, crackers, and fruit for us to enjoy on the porch. It's so beautiful outside, and Victoria is back from the hospital. I thought a little sunshine and delicious food would hit the spot. Would you like to join us?"

"I would love to. In fact, I prepared dinner to bring to you and your lovely wife. It's in the oven right now."

"How thoughtful. I could get used to all these home-cooked meals. I know Victoria appreciates it as well. Thank you. Why don't you stop by whenever you're ready? Victoria is washing up. I'm sure she'll be down soon," he says.

"It's a plan. See you in a few," I tell him.

***

The timer on my phone says the meatloaf has roughly thirty minutes to go. I peek out my front window, and Emilio and Victoria are seated on their porch. Victoria gasps, and Emilio hugs her. Then, they both laugh. I wonder what that's about. After removing my apron, which Ali calls my "Martha Stewart costume," I grab my phone and a few of my children's books and head over.

Victoria's face lights up as I approach, and she waves. This is the happiest I've seen her since she and Emilio arrived. She must be glad to be home from the hospital. Her green velour tracksuit barely covers her belly, and a black baseball cap sits on her head.

"Hi, Gemma," she says as she stands to give me a hug.

"Victoria, you look well. How are you feeling?"

"I'm well. Thanks for asking. Apart from a little mishap in the shower a few minutes ago, of course," she says.

"Uh, oh. You didn't fall, did you?" I ask.

Victoria removes the baseball cap and reveals several bald spots. She puts the cap back on, her cheeks red from embarrassment.

"Oh. Um. So, it was my fault, actually," Emilio admits with a frown on his face. "When we unpacked toiletries the other day, I was the one who put the shower supplies away. I put my hair remover in the shower instead of Victoria's shampoo. The bottles look very similar. I'm so sorry, Victoria."

Victoria chuckles. "And I can see zilch with my contacts out. It turns out it was a case of mistaken bottle identity."

"Your absentminded husband did not pay attention once again," Emilio says.

"That sounds like something I would do. One time I accidentally used an icing tube instead of glue for a project," I tell them. "Let me see your hair again, Victoria."

I touch her hair to see what the damage is and say, "I have a friend who works at the salon downtown. I'm sure she would be happy to fix it up a bit."

Victoria smiles and says, "That's a great idea. I was worried I would have to shave it all off."

"Nonsense. We'll fix it. And I'm sure with your prenatal vitamins, your hair will grow back in no time. What is your natural color anyway?"

Victoria looks embarrassed, and I feel bad I asked. It's only because I can see her roots, and they are not deep black.

"Umm, my hair is naturally chestnut brown," she says. "The color was an experiment."

"I like the black. It suits you. Although chestnut brown is very pretty, too."

"I almost forgot. We have a little gift for you," Victoria says, as she shoos Emilio into the house to retrieve it.

Emilio reappears with a velvet wine bag with blue and gold details. He hands it to me. I undo the delicate drawstring tie to reveal a bottle of 2022 Caymus Vineyards Cabernet Sauvignon.

"Oh, you shouldn't have," I gush. "But I'm glad you did. Once that little boy makes his appearance, we can enjoy this together. What do you say?"

"Yes, I miss wine so much," Victoria admits. "Not drinking might be the hardest part about this pregnancy. I also miss sushi. I can't wait to get my hands on a shrimp tempura roll."

"I almost forgot," I say as I hand her the books. "Dinner is almost ready, but I wanted to give these to you."

Victoria looks at me with the excitement of a small child. She opens the top book: Teddy and the Blue Umbrella. It was the first book I ever wrote about a teddy bear whose umbrella takes him on an adventure through the forest. He meets many friends along the way, such as a purple rabbit and an Arctic polar bear.

"Oh, thank you. This is wonderful," she looks at the cover of each book and takes the artwork in. "We'll go through them tonight. I can read to him before bed. I love these illustrations, Gemma. They're so happy and colorful."

"I can read fine on my own, thank you very much," Emilio says. He laughs at his own joke.

"Not you. The baby," she says, and rolls her eyes at Emilio.

I don't know what it is, but Victoria has come to life since her stay at the hospital. Only a few days ago, she was tentative to talk to anyone. One might say she almost seemed scared. This woman in front of me is bubbly and sweet.

The timer on my phone buzzes, and all three of us jump. Emilio laughs and asks if I need any help in the kitchen.

"Oh, no. You two sit and enjoy yourselves. I will be right back with dinner," I tell them.

As I walk home, I see the mysterious new neighbor in his truck, the trailer no longer attached. His Ford F-250 roars as the engine turns over, and I get goosebumps. My father, who was a police officer, had the same type of truck. We would drive to the lake on weekends. The sound of the engine takes me back to the best memories of my life, and I can't help but wonder if it's a sign. The man pulls out of his driveway and, as he drives past me, waves. He sure is handsome.

# Chapter 15

VICTORIA

Being on the move for the past two months has dramatically added to my anxiety. I'm not the person I once was, but I'm slowly enjoying life again and relearning what it's like to live without fear. Thanks to Emilio. As the days go on, the house at 251 Sycamore Way feels more like home with every step we take over the threshold. And it's not only on Sycamore Way that the people are so friendly; it's everywhere in Laurelville.

Back home, I used yoga and meditation to reset my mind and body after a long day at the hospital. I should begin my practice again to calm my nerves. It's silly for me to think that Jack will find us. He's still back home in the city. There's no way he would track me down to this little town in the middle of nowhere. Even though I believe this in my mind, the ball of anxiety in the pit of my stomach remains steady every day. I'm sure it's a manifestation of the fear that I have accumulated these past months.

Gemma approaches with dinner on a white platter. The platter has three sections, and she peels off the foil cover to reveal slices of meatloaf, creamy mashed potatoes, and green peas. At the sight of the peas, a lump forms in my stomach. Lately, peas make me feel nauseous. Emilio clears the almost empty charcuterie board off the table and carries out clean plates and cutlery.

"It smells heavenly, Gemma. You really didn't have to do this. You've done so much for us already," I tell her.

She flutters her hand at me and says, "Don't be silly. I live for this stuff. Ask anyone. Feeding you gives me immense amounts of joy."

She sits down and serves us each meatloaf and mashed potatoes. When she gets to the peas, I stifle my gag reflex. I press my fingers firmly to my lips.

"Sorry, none for me," I say. I feel bad for refusing, but if I don't, I'll be sick all over the table.

Gemma retracts the spoonful of peas. Her face flushes when she sees the expression on my face.

"Oh, no. Okay, peas are a no. I'm so sorry. I realize now that I never asked you if you have any allergies."

She puts her hand on my shoulder to make sure I'm okay.

I gain my composure and say, "No, no, it's not your fault. I'm not allergic. In fact, before I was pregnant, I loved peas. It must be this little guy who doesn't like them. Emilio and I went to a

Cracker Barrel, and I almost tossed my cookies when I saw the peas. So weird."

I rub my belly, and Gemma nods. "Are there any other foods that don't agree with you?"

"No, other than that, I like the same foods I always have."

Gemma nods. "Do you crave many foods?"

"Mm, not really," I say. "Sometimes I'll see a commercial on TV for fast food and crave that, but the urge typically goes away once the commercial is over."

"Uh, excuse me. Not really? Who was it that made me get up at 2:00 a.m. for beef jerky? We're lucky they sell it at all gas stations," Emilio says.

I laugh. "I forgot about that. That was only one time."

"Three times! It was three times. And always in the middle of the night. You would have thought I would have learned to buy more than one package after the second time."

"He must take after his daddy," I say. My face burns red right after I say it, but Emilio doesn't miss a beat.

"Yes, I do love beef jerky. But not in the middle of the night."

He reaches over, holds my hand, and squeezes it. I take a deep breath.

"Are you okay?" Gemma asks, a look of worry on her face.

"Yes, it's a little bit of indigestion. It comes and goes throughout the day, whether I've eaten or not," I tell her.

"Have you tried the Italian antacid?" Gemma asks.

"Yes, thank you so much, Gemma. I forgot to tell you that I tried it, and it works like a charm."

We dig into the meal, and I groan as I savor the delicious food.

"So," Gemma says, "Have you seen the new guy who moved in down the block? He's next door to Seamus and Darby."

"The guy in the blue truck?" Emilio asks.

"That's the one. He's quite handsome. He's tall and very muscley," Gemma giggles, and I can tell she might have a little crush on the new guy.

"Oh, where is he from?" I ask.

"I'm not sure. As far as I know, no one on the block has met him yet. Well, except for Fiona, probably. She sells or rents out every house on this block. She owns the one he moved into. The Hadley family used to live there, but they moved earlier this year. Ali, Darby, and I saw the new guy pull into his driveway with a U-Haul the other day."

"Will you make him a welcome basket?" I ask.

"Probably," she says. "I might need a little more intel on him, though. Fiona tells all the neighbors about anyone new to Sycamore. Ali said Fiona told us about the new guy at the last girls' night, but neither Darby nor I recall it. Too much wine, I guess. It's fine. I'll send Fiona a text later to get the scoop."

"I would be happy to help you with the basket, if you'd like," I hear myself say. Gemma's warm energy draws me to her. When I'm around her, I feel safe. Normally, I would never volunteer to make a welcome basket.

Gemma beams. "Yes! That would be so fun. How about I come get you tomorrow, and we'll go shopping?"

I smile and say yes. Gift baskets are harmless, right? Plus, this might be what I need to take my mind off Jack.

***

The next day, Emilio leaves early to find a job. His plan is to look over the job board at Fiona's office complex and perhaps chat with a few people at the local businesses. Gemma drops by at noon, and we grab a bite before shopping for the new guy's welcome basket. She takes us to a darling bookshop and café where I order a chicken salad and strawberry lemonade. Gemma orders a slice of mushroom and spinach quiche and a latté.

"I love your dress," Gemma says. I look down at the yellow floral summer dress I threw on earlier. It's one of the few items I own that I don't find constricting.

"Oh, thanks," I tell her. "So, what did you find out about the new guy?"

Gemma pulls a little notebook out of her purse and flips it open.

I giggle and then say, "You and Emilio are so much alike. He carries around a little notebook like that to make lists in."

"Smart man," Gemma says. "That's exactly what I do. Okay, so hot guy down the street list."

I take in the information as she reads the list.

"The new guy's name is Keith. He's in his mid-thirties. He's a contractor. And he moved here from somewhere up north. He's quite handsome. I added that last observation myself. He reminds me of the guy from the G.I. Joe cartoon. My dad and I used to watch that cartoon together on Saturday mornings."

I interrupt her mid-list. This guy sounds a lot like Jack.

"Did Fiona tell you where up north? And why did he move here?"

"Okay, so get this. Promise not to tell anyone."

Little goosebumps rise on my arm. The new guy has a secret.

"He's newly single," Gemma says, then giggles. She reminds me of a giddy schoolgirl who has a crush on the cutest boy in class.

"Oh, okay. Why can't we tell anyone?" I ask, confused.

"I mean, don't tell anyone because I call dibs on this one. Oh, don't mind me. I'm so silly. It's not really a secret, secret. You look like you've seen a ghost. Are you okay?"

"Um, yeah. Of course," I say, trying to play it off. "Do you know what happened to his ex?"

"I don't know. Fiona didn't say. Maybe it was a bad breakup, so he decided on a change of scenery. Who knows?"

I change the subject. "So, any idea on what he likes or dislikes?"

"Fiona wasn't too sure, but she said he was active military several years ago. Maybe that's why they broke up. Since he's single, he'd probably love a home-cooked meal. Maybe a chicken pot pie? Martha Stewart's recipe is to die for. It's one hundred percent from scratch. And what about some masculine stuff for the gift basket? Sexy stuff for a sexy guy. What do you think?"

"How about Shepherd's Pie instead? I think a masculine guy like him might like it better than chicken pot pie," I suggest. I have an idea.

Gemma considers this, then says, "Shepherd's Pie. I like that."

Gemma and I enter a small boutique with home décor. We choose a few novelty items that we think a guy like Keith would like—a black candle, a set of kitchen towels, and a set of coasters made from petrified wood. Afterward, we cross the street to the grocery store to pick up ingredients for the Shepherd's pie and a bottle of red wine.

I'm picking through the bunches of carrots when I hear a female voice call out, "Hey! I thought that it was you. How have you been?"

My first instinct is to run, but my body freezes up instead. *Is she speaking to me?* I don't recognize the voice. I don't dare turn my head to see where Gemma is. I take a deep breath and turn around to see a lady I have never met before in my life.

"Oh, I'm so sorry. From behind, you look exactly like my friend Danielle. Clearly, you're not her," she says with a little laugh, then gives a little wave as if we can both forget what happened. My heart takes a minute to stop pounding.

Gemma arrives and places a pink package from the butcher and a few cans of tomato paste into the cart.

"Who was that?" she asks. "Do you know her?"

"No, mistaken identity. She thought I was her friend."

"You okay?"

"Mm, hmm. She just startled me."

Deep down, I was so scared I almost peed myself thinking someone from back home had found me.

# Chapter 16



KEITH

I swipe my brow on my sleeve and backpedal to examine the deck. Not bad. This old house will need a lot of tender loving care, but it's got good bones. I promised Fiona I'd fix it up to be rentable by next summer. With any luck, I'll be long gone before that. My beer has gone warm, so I go inside to dump it when the doorbell rings. It must be Fiona.

I'm surprised to find the woman I saw on my way to the hardware store on my porch. She's quite pretty, and if I'm correct, we're about the same age. In the woman's arms is a large picnic basket, and a large German Shepherd is patiently sitting next to her. He reminds me of my childhood dog, Lars.

"Hello," I say.

"Hi, there," she says, her cheeks pink. "I'm Gemma. I live three doors down. And this is Chester. We want to welcome you to the neighborhood with some treats."

I take the basket from her outstretched arms. I'm not sure what to say other than thank you. Small talk is not my strong suit.

"This is very nice of you. Thanks," I say, awkwardly. "I'm Keith. Would you like to come in?"

"Oh, no. That's okay. I'm sure you're still settling in. There's homemade Shepherd's pie in the basket, so you'll want to re-frigerate that right away. Everything else is non-perishable, so..." she trails off, and I wonder if she's a little uncomfortable around someone of my stature. At six-foot-five, I can come across as intimidating.

"Shepherd's pie is my favorite. Thank you so much. And sorry, I'm bad with names. What did you say your name was again? Gina?" I ask, embarrassed. Now *my* face turns red.

"Gemma. My name is Gemma." She smiles. An awkward silence follows.

"Okay, we'd better go," Gemma says. "I'm sure you'll love it here on Sycamore. Enjoy the goodies."

She turns around and heads down my porch stairs. Chester follows her.

"Wait," I say, and she turns around. "I don't know anyone here except for Fiona. Are you sure I can't tempt you with a cold beer and some of this delicious food you brought?"

I can tell she's contemplating whether to trust the new stranger in town. I am a little sweaty, after all. She doesn't seem to mind, though, because she smiles and says, "Well, okay.

Maybe we'll come in for a minute. Chester and I love getting to know our neighbors."

I stand aside to let her and Chester in.

"I used to have a dog," I tell her as I grab us each a cold beer. "His name was Lars. He was a Malinois."

"Aww, that's so sweet. Was he your childhood dog?" she asks.

"Yeah. My dad was in the National Guard, so he was away a lot. He brought Lars home when he was only a puppy, and we trained him together. Lars was an amazing dog. He could do tricks and knew how to protect our family in case of an intruder. Lars lived until he was sixteen. I was twenty-two."

My eyes water a little as I think about Lars and my dad. My dad was a brute, and training Lars is the only happy memory I have of him. Those memories belong to the past, though. I don't need to rehash them to Gemma. I look at Chester, who is well-trained. I wish I had treats for him.

"Here," I say, as I pull out a kitchen chair. "Have a seat. I'll serve up the pie."

Gemma sits down and takes a swig of her beer. I'm glad I bought the good IPA instead of the usual crap I drink. I fill a bowl of water for Chester, and he eagerly laps it up. I give him a scratch on the head when he's done.

"Thirsty boy, eh?" I say as he licks my forearm and gives me his paw to shake.

"Don't be fooled by his friendly demeanor. Chester is a trained attack dog. My dad was a police officer and worried about me being a single gal and all. He felt that I was vulnerable, so I promised him I would get a dog. I had a retired K9 named Butch for a while. When he passed away a few years ago, I found Chester. He's my best friend." At that, Chester walks over to Gemma and looks up at her. She laughs. "It's okay, Chester. Let's hang out here for a little bit with our new friend."

Chester takes the hint and lies down. The Shepherd's pie is still warm as I take it out of the basket and listen to Gemma talk about her past. There's a familiarity I find in Gemma. I dish up the pie and set a plate in front of her.

"Thank you," she says. "So, you said Shepherd's pie was a favorite of yours. Did you eat it as a kid?"

"No, my ex introduced me to it. It became my favorite dish. I'm a meat and potatoes guy," I tell her.

She nods and takes a bite. I do the same. The food is at the perfect temperature.

"This is fantastic," I say. "It's probably the best meal I've had in the past several months."

"Months?" she says. "What have you been up to?"

"Mainly packing stuff up for the move. And working. As a contractor, I eat on the go and on-site. Fast food becomes your new cuisine if you don't have someone at home to make you real food."

"I don't remember the last time I had fast food," she says. "I guess that means I'll be bringing you over more home-cooked meals."

"I would love that," I tell her, and I almost forget that I'm only here temporarily. I could get used to this neighborhood. And to Gemma's sweet smile.

# Chapter 17

Gemma

I'm in a creative mood after my visit with Keith, so I bake up a storm of cakes, cookies, scones—you name it. I even make some homemade peanut butter dog treats for Chester, which he happily gobbles up. Later, Victoria and I walk to Ali's house with armfuls of goodies.

"Helloooo!" I say as we enter.

Sydney runs up to me and takes the fabric shopping bag I am about to drop. Luckily, it only has the muffins in it and not the wine.

"Hi, Auntie Gemma and Auntie Victoria. Welcome to our house," she says, holding her arms out as if to show us the place. She's adorable with her blonde pigtails and the little dimple in her left cheek, a trait she had even as an infant.

Victoria and I laugh in unison.

"I like your hair, Auntie Victoria," Sydney says.

Victoria touches her hair, which is now in a pixie cut.

"Oh, thank you, Syd," Victoria says, then turns to me. "She is quite the little hostess. I hope my little guy is that friendly. Articulate children always impress me."

"Well, I know I don't have any children of my own," I say. "But I've noticed that the children who are talked to and read to the most seem to have the best vocabularies."

"That makes sense. Because they're able to use their words to describe things," Victoria says as she lays out the goodies on Ali's counter. Sydney hops up on a barstool to help.

Ali treads down the stairs and gives me and Victoria each a hug, then compliments Victoria on her new haircut. She says to Sydney, "Thank you for helping, Syd. Do you want to go over to Brodie's house to play or stay here with us?"

"I wanna stay here with you guys. Did you see all the stuff Auntie Gemma brought?"

Ali laughs. "That's my girl. Bribed by sweets."

Darby and Penelope arrive soon after. Darby has Ramona with her, so it's perfect that Sydney decided to stay. Ramona looks up to Sydney like a big sister, even though they're only two years apart. Once we're all settled on Ali's back patio with wine, a glass of Italian soda for Victoria, and small plates of snacks, the conversation begins.

"No, Fiona tonight?" Penelope asks.

"Nope, she has an early morning tomorrow. Brokers tour over in Locke City," I tell them. "She said next time for sure, though."

"So, tell us about the new guy," Darby says.

I give them the scoop on Keith. Of course, everyone interrupts with questions, so it takes forever to get to the fact that he can do handyman work around the neighborhood. The ladies gasp in excitement.

"I have so many projects that Brooks doesn't have time for," Ali says. "I swear, I never see my husband. If I didn't have you ladies to hang out with, I'd probably go stir crazy."

"And me," Sydney chimes in. "You have me, too."

Everyone in the room melts at Sydney's comment, and Ali grabs her and pulls her in close. "I love you, Syd. Of course. We have each other. Mama and Sydney forever and ever," Ali gives Sydney a little peck on the nose before Sydney and Ramona run off to Sydney's room.

"I know what you mean. Seamus isn't really too much of a fix-it guy, plus he's never home. It'll be handy to have someone on the block who you can call to replace a lightbulb," Darby says, and we all laugh.

Victoria is the only one who stays silent, as if she is off in another world. I squeeze her hand and quietly ask, "You okay?" She snaps out of it and smiles.

"Mm hmm," she says. "I was making a mental list of the projects we could have for him. Emilio is handy, but sometimes there could be a two-man job he needs help with. I'm in no shape to be the second man."

She points to her belly, and we all laugh in agreement.

"Plus, he's hot," Penelope says.

"I call dibs," I hear myself say, my face hot with embarrassment as I say it.

"It only makes sense, Gemma. All of us are married. We can still look, though. I mean, have you seen his butt? I wonder what gym he works out at," Penelope says.

"Well, he *is* ex-military," I tell them.

# Chapter 18

Victoria

"Are you sure you're okay?" Gemma asks me as we walk home from Ali's house.

"Yes, I'm fine," I say. I am doing my best not to grill her about Keith. The way Gemma has described this new guy on the block sounds so much like Jack, it's got me spooked. "So, did the new guy say what branch of the military he was in?"

"I think he said the National Guard. Or no, I think that was his dad. Army, maybe?"

I nod. The hair on the back of my neck stands up.

"Hmm. And he has an ex-wife?"

"Wife or girlfriend. I didn't ask. He had a dog when he was a kid. A Malinois named Lars."

"And his favorite dish is Shepherd's Pie?"

"Yep! That was a great suggestion. I'm glad I made that instead of the chicken pot pie. How did you know?" Gemma asks me.

I shrug. "I assumed if he was a big, strong guy, he would want red meat instead of chicken."

"You were so right," Gemma says as we reach my porch. "I'll think of other manly dishes to make him. And your hair looks so good. I told you Samantha would work her magic on it."

I touch my hair. The short, pixie cut doesn't really suit my personality, but hides the large chunks that fell out, including the strands in the front. Samantha, Gemma's hairdresser friend, cut and styled it so that the longer strands covered up the missing pieces. My hair used to be a deep chestnut brown. I miss it. I wonder what my baby's hair color will be. Brown like mine or dirty blond like Jack's?

"Thanks, Gemma. Her hands sure did work their magic," I say. "I'm less self-conscious about it now."

"Plus, I'm sure it will grow back in no time," Gemma says. "You're so pretty you can pull off any style, though."

She leans in for a hug, and we say goodbye. I really like Gemma. She's like the sister I never had.

***

Although it's close to 9:00 p.m., Emilio is at the stove stirring a lemony and garlicky concoction. It smells divine. I stop and take a whiff.

Emilio says, "Chicken Piccata. I stopped by the store on my way home to pick up some fresh herbs and lemons. They really make a difference."

The aroma is so intoxicating that I almost forget about the conversation at girls' night. I fill a glass of water and sit down. I recap the information Gemma told me about Keith. I emphasize the uncanniness of what he looks like—tall with green eyes worthy of hypnotizing anyone with estrogen. It must be Jack.

Emilio rolls his eyes at me.

"What?" I ask. "Emilio. What if Jack found us? What if he's watching us?"

I shudder.

"I think we should leave. Go somewhere farther away. Maybe across the country," I say, the panic in my gut.

"Wait a minute, don't you think you're getting a little carried away? You said this man is a contractor and a handyman. Does that sound like Jack to you?"

"No, but he was a mechanic. And I think he could build stuff."

"Jack might have been able to build a birdfeeder. Or hang a picture on the wall. Other than that, I have never seen him build or fix items around your home or the shop. Have you?" Emilio takes my hands in his. "If it were Jack, don't you think he would be at our door by now?"

He has a point. I try to recall Jack's handyman skills, but I draw a blank. We lived in an apartment, so we only had minor repairs. Maintenance fixed anything that was more than a lightbulb change or a smoke alarm battery. It still doesn't change the fact that this guy has so much in common with Jack. After all, I was the one who introduced him to Shepherd's Pie.

# Chapter 19



KEITH

They say patience is a virtue. It's a trait that I've never seemed to have much of, but my service in the military helped with that. So far, keeping surveillance on Sycamore Way has been an easy task, but then again, it might very well be the calm before the storm. When I first agreed to move here, Fiona mapped out the neighborhood for me so I could keep track of who lives where. From the second floor of my house, I can see most of the neighborhood.

I sit in the front bedroom with my long-range binoculars. The lights are off while I make my observations. This has been my routine every night since I arrived. The house across the street has its curtains open, revealing a man, a woman, and a little girl at their dinner table—Brooks, Ali, and Sydney. Most nights, it's only Ali and Sydney. The lights are out at Fiona's house, and I assume she's in for the night. Her car is parked out front. The lights are on in the yellow house next door to Fiona. Although my house is several yards away, I can hear the echo of laughter from children and attempts by their parents to shush them. This sounds about right. According to the map, that's Penelope and Freddy's house. And they have two boys, Brodie and Oakley. I move to the back bedroom, where I have a clear view of the master bedroom next door. The woman, Darby, is undressing, and her husband, Seamus, the big, burly redhead, comes over and wraps his arms around her. He looks out the window, and although I know he can't see me, I move back into the hallway. I don't need to be pegged by my neighbors as a voyeur. The lights are off at Gemma's house and at the house of the new neighbors, Victoria and Emilio.

Although I haven't formally met any of the neighbors other than Gemma and Fiona, I know I'll have to work on it and integrate myself into this neighborhood. Timing is everything. My mission is simple. Protect the neighborhood at any cost. I turn on my laptop and click on a graphic design program. Here goes.

# Chapter 20

VICTORIA

I slide the closet door open and remove my white sneakers, my tan crossbody bag, my black puffy coat, and my favorite cuffed jeans. Each piece hides a bit of my stash. I take the crisp bills out and count them. Five thousand six hundred and eighty dollars. Not bad, but I'll need to find a job as soon as the baby is born. This money won't last forever, and I don't want to dip into the trust fund money that I've saved for the baby. For now, we're in a good place, money-wise. Emilio says he will support us and that I can stay at home with the baby for as long as I'd like, but I'm not someone who depends on others. I've always been self-sufficient and have pulled my own weight. Plus, Emilio has already done so much for the baby and me.

Emilio arrives back home at around 4:00 p.m. I'm excited to hear about his day.

"Hello! I'm home," he announces as I hobble down the stairs to greet him.

He carries a white bag with handles and holds it out to me as I approach.

"For you," he says, a grin on his face.

"Hey, I thought you were job hunting. Instead, you were out buying me treats?" I chide.

"Look inside," Emilio says. "This was part of the process."

I open the bag and pull out a small pink bakery box. My heart skips a beat, and giddiness washes over me. *Is this what I think it is?*

The box reveals three perfect cannoli; each one a crispy shell stuffed with creamy ricotta. Back home, we had an Italian bakery in North Beach. I fell in love with the delicious treats the first time Emilio brought them over. I peek in the box; one has pistachios, another mini chocolate chips, and the last one maraschino cherries.

"Where did you find these?" I ask as I take a bite of the pistachio one. I hold out the box to Emilio, but he shakes his head.

"I went to Locke City on my job search and found a little Italian bakery. I thought you would like them. I already ate two while I was talking to the owner."

"These remind me of the ones you used to bring over. They're so fresh," I say, powdered sugar now everywhere. "Thank you."

"You have a little right here," he says, as he wipes my chin off with his thumb.

I set the cannoli down.

"So, how was your job search?"

"I got a job," he says, and I wait for him to tell me more. "At the bakery."

I look at him as if he's kidding. For as long as I've known Emilio, he's been a mechanic. I give him a look of skepticism and surprise.

"I know it's different," he says. "But, you know how I love to bake. I figured, if one day Jack did find us, he wouldn't look for me in a bakery. He would look for me at an auto repair shop or car dealership. And he would look for you in a clinic or a hospital."

He has a point. And a job is better than no job. I don't ask him how much it pays. It bothers me that Locke City is forty minutes away. *What if I go into labor and he doesn't make it back in time?*

Again, Emilio reads my mind. He pulls a phone out of his pocket. It's an iPhone. My eyes light up.

"Okay, okay, before you get too excited, we need to lay down some ground rules for safety reasons. We've come this far, and the baby is almost here."

I am as attentive as a sixteen-year-old who has been given the keys to a brand-new car by her parents. I nod as Emilio goes through the list of dos and don'ts.

"No faces or location on social media. In fact, no posts what-soever. We can use it to stalk our friends to see what they're up to. Also, don't call anyone we know from back home."

"Even Scarlett?"

"Especially Scarlett. I'm sure Jack hopes that she'll give up your location. She can't know. I know you trust her, but Jack is very manipulative."

I nod. He's right. But it's killing me not to talk to my best friend. Back home, we spoke every day. I saw a public phone in downtown Laurelville the other day and thought about it, but it would show my area code. I took a chance the one time I called her when we were on the road.

"What do you think?" he asks me.

"I think you're right," I say. "We have to stay safe."

"Gemma put her number in our phones and Ali's and Dar-by's," he says, and I feel a tinge of happiness run through my body. I have friends now.

"That was fast. You only bought the phones today."

Emilio laughs. "Yes, but when I pulled into the driveway right now, Gemma saw me. I showed her the phones, and she wanted to be the first to put her number in yours so you guys could text. She said something about *manly* suggestions."

Emilio shrugs, and I laugh. As if on cue, my phone dings with a text. Only, it's not Gemma. It's Ali. The text reads: Hey! Gemma gave me your number. It's Ali. Sydney and I want to see if you and Emilio would like to come over for dinner tomorrow.

6:15 p.m.? Gemma's coming too. Brooks will be home so he and Emilio can hang out.

My first text on my new phone. I don't even think or ask Emilio before I answer: Yes! We would love to!

I get a thumbs-up emoji in response and an answer back that reads: See you soon!

# Chapter 21

Gemma

The pot of Bolognese simmers on the stove, and the aroma of Italian herbs magically takes over the kitchen. I twirl around in my kitchen as I cook, and Chester stares at me as if I've grown another head. Keith asked me out to dinner like a gentleman, but I insisted on making him my authentic Pasta Bolognese instead. The thought of spending time with him again gives me butterflies. The Bolognese recipe comes from my great-great-grandmother and has two secret ingredients that I will take to the grave (unless I have children, of course). I've never met a soul whose eyes haven't rolled back in their head from the savory meat sauce.

A voice yells out as I stroll down to Keith's house, "You look like a cross between Mary Poppins and Julie Andrews." I look around and see Ali at her front door, laughing hysterically. I blush as I laugh with her and yell, "That's not nice!"

She closes the door, but I can still hear her laugh, and I chuckle too. *What would I do without friends like Ali?*

Keith answers the door with a nervous look on his face. I'm glad I'm not the only one. He dons a black polo shirt and black jeans, and I'm dressed in a simple floral dress with nude flats and the delicate gold bracelet my dad gave me for my fifteenth birthday.

"You look beautiful," he says as he takes the food from me and takes a whiff. "And this smells out of this world."

"If there's one thing I excel at, it's food," I say with a chuckle.

"I believe that. I can't imagine anything better than that Shepherd's Pie," he says as he places the salad, pasta, and sauce on the table with the serving utensils. He places an open bottle of Chianti on the table.

Keith serves us heaping portions of food and fills our glasses. "I can tell this meal will knock my socks off," he says.

I laugh and watch as he takes his first bite of pasta.

"Wow," he says as he shakes his head in awe. "Mm...mm...mm."

"Thank you," I say, beaming.

We sit in silence for a few minutes. Keith devours the hot food. His pasta bowl is three-quarters empty when he puts his utensils down.

"Umm, Gemma?" he says.

"Mm, hmm?" I say. I take a sip of wine.

"Would you mind giving me your opinion on something?"

I raise an eyebrow. *What could that be?*

Keith slides his chair back to stand and reaches for a piece of paper on the counter. He hands it to me. KEITH'S HANDYMAN SERVICES, it reads, followed by a list of the types of jobs he has experience with and his phone number and address. There's a little cartoon in the upper right corner of a guy holding a wrench and a plunger, which makes me laugh. I read down his list of skills and am impressed that he knows how to do electrical and plumbing work.

"This is great. I'm sure a lot of people could use your services around here," I tell him. "You're much better looking than this guy, though. Don't sell yourself short."

Keith laughs, then says, "You think it's okay?"

"Yes, it's perfect."

"I'm glad you think so. Because I printed out about fifty of them," he chuckles.

"We should go for a walk after dinner and put them in people's mailboxes. We can do Sycamore and a few of the nearby streets."

Keith nods and takes another bite of Bolognese, smiling as he does so. A dimple appears on his left cheek. "Gemma, that sounds like a great idea. Thank you."

***

Our stomachs are full of pasta and wine, so it feels good to get up and walk. After dinner, we stop by my place to collect Chester. He loves sniffing at the different plants and bushes along the way. As we pass Victoria and Emilio's house, a shadow appears behind the sheer curtains in the front window. I assume it must be Victoria or Emilio, so I wave. But the curtain moves slightly, and in an instant, the shadow disappears, sending shivers down my spine.

I forget about it once we move on to the next street, Oak Terrace. Once again, the conversation flows easily between Keith and I as we talk about many topics—from food to our childhoods. It turns out that Keith has quite a sense of humor. He has a younger brother whom he has always kept out of trouble. As a teenager, his militant father wasn't home much, so it was a household of pranks and burp and fart jokes. I laugh when he tells me this because it's very opposite from the childhood I experienced as an only child and the daughter of a stay-at-home mom and a police officer dad.

My mother had several miscarriages after me, so she and my father stopped trying. My parents doted on me. My mother taught me how to cook, bake, and do many household hacks. She passed away from ovarian cancer when I was in college at the Rhode Island School of Design. I dropped out of school in my second year to come back home and take care of my dad. He was diagnosed with early-onset dementia, and I didn't know how much longer I would have with him. My dad was the one who taught me how to change a tire and the oil in my car. He also taught me self-defense and what self-worth meant. "Never settle, Gemma," he would say. "You deserve the best."

After I moved back to Laurelville, I created children's books. At first, it was a few doodles to keep my dad entertained and laughing. I ended up with a complete cast of cartoon characters I would later use in my books. My dad passed away only six months after I moved back from college. Even though he had dementia, I knew the real reason he died was from heartbreak. He and my mom were high school sweethearts. I've never seen two people so much in love.

A tear in Keith's eye appears as I tell him my story. He reaches over and takes my hand in his. A calming warmth emanates from his hand to mine.

"That was a long time ago. I'm fine now. It was hard, you know?" I say, then turn the subject back to him. "So, do you keep in touch with your brother and parents?"

He lets my hand go and says, "Not so much. My mom passed away when I was ten. My dad disappeared a little over nine years ago."

A lump forms in my throat.

"Disappeared?" I ask, but my voice comes out as a whisper.

"Without a trace," he says.

# Chapter 22

Victoria

"Emilio! Emilio!" I shout as I run up the stairs as fast as I can. My heart is pounding, but I can't stop. I need to get to Emilio.

"What's wrong?" Emilio's eyes are big as he exits the bathroom, his arms out wide to catch me.

"It's not him. It's not Jack," I say, catching my breath.

"What? Who is not Jack? Slow down," Emilio says. "Explain."

"The new guy in the blue truck. He and Gemma walked by. She waved, so I think she saw me standing in the window. I saw his face, and it's one hundred percent not Jack."

It's as if a boulder has been lifted off my shoulders. Emilio hugs me and stares into my eyes.

"I know you said it wasn't him, but I had to see it with my own eyes," I tell him.

Emilio drags me into the bedroom and pats the bed. *What is he doing? Is he making a move? Now?* Tentatively, I sit down. He sets down Gemma's bag of books on the bed and pulls one out. Then, he sits down next to me. I'm such an idiot. In the two months on the go, never once did Emilio try to make a move on me. *Why would he do it now? Am I losing my mind?*

"It's important for the baby and you to relax. We don't want him to be a stress case like his mama," Emilio laughs. "Now that you've proven the new neighbor isn't Jack, you can finally relax."

"You're right," I say. "And Emilio?"

"Yes?"

"Thank you."

Emilio reads Gemma's book about a teddy bear out loud, his voice calm and soothing. Before I know it, I drift into a deep sleep.

***

I wake up the next morning, and my energy levels are through the roof. I didn't even get up in the middle of the night to pee like I often do. I slip into the bathroom to relieve my bladder and then go downstairs to see what Emilio is up to. A note on the kitchen counter reads:

*Be back in a few. Went next door to help Gemma. -E*

Next to the note sits a latte with a happy smile written in black Sharpie on the lid. I take a sip of the latte and savor it.

Emilio really spoils me. I walk over to the front window and see a large white delivery truck backed into Gemma's driveway, but there is no sign of either of them.

I go back into the kitchen and sit on a barstool, sipping my latte for a few minutes before the worry creeps in. Then I hear it. The sound of a cackling exhaust system. I look at the front door. It's locked. As quickly as I can, I slide down from the barstool and crawl over to the front window. The sound is gone. *Could that have been Jack's car? Has he found us? The delivery truck has left, and there's still no sign of Gemma or Emilio. Where are they?*

I look through the kitchen window directly across from Gemma's and see Emilio laughing. I open the window and yell, "Emilio!" He looks up and waves me over. I shake my head. There's no way I'm going out there. *What if Jack comes back?*

I hear Emilio's key turn in the front door.

"Hey! The sleepyhead is awake. Come over to Gemma's with me," he says.

I tell Emilio about the sound, and he says, "I was outside a minute ago, Victoria. Jack didn't drive by. It must have been the delivery truck you heard driving away."

*Am I that paranoid? I know the sound of Jack's car. How could I mistake a delivery truck for a modified Subaru exhaust system?* A wave of relief washes over me. Although I'm in my robe and slippers, I head over to Gemma's with Emilio.

Gemma's garage door is open, as is the door that leads into her house. I peek my head in and call out, "Hello?"

"In here!" I hear Gemma yell. "C'mon in!"

I follow her voice into the house, Emilio right behind me, to find Gemma and Keith in the living room. I'm a little embarrassed to be dressed in a robe and slippers and wrap my robe a little tighter around my midsection.

Gemma comes over to me and gives me a squeeze.

"Thank you for letting me borrow Emilio. This was a two-man job," she says. A huge cardboard box sits on the floor, and Keith slices it open with a box cutter.

"Victoria, this is Keith, our new neighbor. I don't think you two have met yet. Keith, this is Victoria, Emilio's wife."

"Nice to meet you, Victoria," Keith says, then turns to Gemma. "That sucker was heavy. There was no way you were getting this in here by yourself."

"Likewise. I've heard a lot about you," I say. Seeing Keith up close, he looks a little like Jack. No wonder Gemma is so attracted to him. I turn to Gemma and say, "So, what's in the box?"

Gemma beams. "It's my new drafting table. I've been creating from my kitchen table this whole time, and I thought it was time to treat myself to a real desk. My editor gave me an advance on the next five books."

"That's fantastic, Gemma," I tell her. "You deserve it."

"And for helping, I have a little treat for you two," she says, heading for the kitchen. She comes back with two lunch-sized brown paper bags.

"I baked yesterday, so it's a hodgepodge of cookies and other pastries."

Keith and Emilio's eyes light up like little boys.

"I could get used to this," Keith says as he opens the bag and takes a cookie out.

"Me too," Emilio agrees.

***

I wrap the wooden charcuterie board in plastic, careful not to let the contents slide around. It's all about presentation with a board like this. Every slice of meat and cheese is arranged into neat rows, small clusters of red and green grapes separating them.

"Ready?" Emilio says. He grabs the bottles of Sauvignon Blanc and blood orange sparkling water out of the refrigerator and places them into a shopping bag.

Once at Ali's, we're greeted by a very peppy Sydney whose ponytail swings and pink dress swooshes as she leads Emilio and me to the kitchen. We are greeted by Ali, Brooks, and Gemma, who sip on beverages while chatting. Brooks shakes Emilio's hand and offers him a drink in the living room. Emilio is enthusiastic as he gives his undivided attention to Brooks. The two of them chat away as Brooks shows Emilio his whiskey collection.

"Omg, Brooks will talk Emilio's ear off. He loves his whiskey. He'll probably move on to finance or stocks after that," Ali says, as she rolls her eyes.

"That's fine. I'm sure Emilio welcomes it. He's very social. So, where did you and Brooks meet?" I ask her.

"Funny enough, I was coming out of a terrible relationship. I left my hometown, my friends, and my family to recreate myself. I ended up finding a job as an administrative assistant for a finance company in Carlsbad. Within a month, I met Brooks when he was transferred in from the East Coast. He was unlike anyone I had ever met before. He comes off as this serious guy, and some people might even call him a little douchey. It's all an act, though. That's how they are in the finance world," Ali explains.

"So, what made you fall in love with him?" I ask.

"He was the only one in the office to ever call me by my name, ask me if I'd like a coffee when the assistants did coffee runs, and make sure that someone walked me to my car if I was leaving the office late. I felt safe with him. We only dated about two months before I found out I was pregnant with Sydney."

"Wow, that was fast. It appears like it all ended up for the best, though. Sydney is such a sweet girl."

Ali nods, and a look that I can't pinpoint washes over her. "She's my everything. And she loves her daddy as much as I do. We're safe here."

Our gaze is taken to the living room where Brooks' six-foot-five-inch frame is bent over Sydney, who is bopping up and down. She has a teacup in her hand, her stuffed polar bear tucked under her other arm, and clinks her cup to her dad's whiskey glass. Brooks kisses her on the top of her head and says, "That's some good tea, Syd." Sydney giggles and then rushes off to play elsewhere.

"So, what made you and Brooks move to Laurelville?" I ask, then say. "Sorry, I hope I'm not asking too many questions."

"No, no, of course not. Don't be silly. Ask away. We loved the city but wanted to raise Sydney in a quieter environment. Brooks met Fiona at a networking event in San Diego, and she told him about Laurelville. I don't know how she did it, but she convinced him that small-town living is the way to go. I love it here. Brooks spends half of his week in San Diego and half of it here with Syd and me. He works remotely when he's here."

I nod and say, "That's why we moved here, too. It's comfortable. And safe."

"Very safe," she agrees.

Brooks and Emilio fire up the barbecue. Ali, Gemma, and I carry platters of chicken, salmon, steak, and assorted veggies. Sydney helps set the table.

"I love your setup," I tell Ali. She and Brooks have two white picnic benches in one long row. Each table has a Hawaiian-themed umbrella in the middle and matching placemats.

"Thanks," she says. "This is our summer theme. In the fall and winter, we change it out for a more earth-toned theme."

"Makes sense to me," Gemma says, and I nod in agreement. I picture what it will be like when Emilio and I decorate the house and backyard. We'll be able to host neighborhood get-togethers, too.

"I've never had a whole house or yard to decorate before," I tell them. "Maybe once the baby is born, you two could help me with the decor."

You would have thought Gemma and Ali had won the lottery.

"Yes! We would love to come over and help. Your house is the cutest. Have you thought about how you want to decorate the baby's room yet?" Gemma asks.

"Actually, Fiona decorated it before we moved in," I tell them. "It has an airplane motif."

"Oh, wow. That is so, Fiona. You know how she is. She always wants to stick her nose in everyone's business."

"It's a bit tacky, she did it without asking first," Ali says.

"I guess. But I'm sure it was with the best intentions," Gemma says.

"If it were me, I would want to decorate my baby's room myself."

Gemma rolls her eyes. "Admit it, Ali. You're jealous she didn't decorate Sydney's room before you moved in.

There's an awful silence before Gemma, and I read the look on Ali's face.

"Wait, did she?" Gemma asks, breaking the silence.

"To be honest, I completely forgot about it until now. Fiona sold us the house, of course. Sydney's room was decorated in pink and purple bunnies, which I thought was presumptuous of Fiona. Why would she think it was necessary to decorate my baby's room?" Ali says with a flash of anger in her eyes.

"Are you sure it wasn't leftover from the past owners?" Gemma asks, trying to neutralize the situation.

"Positive. I could smell the fresh paint when we did the walk-through. Brooks and I repainted the room eggshell white and had an artist come in to paint a jungle animal mural," Ali says, shaking her head in disgust. "I know you adore Fiona, Gemma, but she can really be pushy. I'm glad she's not my mother-in-law. Can you imagine?"

"I think she means well, though," Gemma says. "She's never mentioned having any kids of her own, so maybe it's her motherly instinct that comes out when a new family moves in."

"You always think the best of everyone, Gemma. It's one of your best qualities. I can be a bit bitter. Bad things in the past, you know?"

"Uh, not really. Anytime I bring up your past, you change the subject," Gemma says.

Ali laughs. "Okay, you got me there, friend. One day I'll tell you about my crazy, sordid past."

"Promise?"

"Promise," Ali says as Sydney bolts into the room with her stuffed polar bear.

"No bunnies for that little one, her favorite lovey is the polar bear I gave her," Gemma says, and before I can ask, she says, "And yes, I gave you the same exact polar bear that Syd has. I call it the kids of Sycamore Way theme. Ramona, Brodie, and Oakley all have one too."

Ali rolls her eyes, "You are such a Martha Stewart, Gemma."

"Hey, Martha's cool. She survived prison, *and* she hangs out with Snoop Dogg."

"You two are too much," I say. "I love it. And I'm sure this little guy will love his polar bear as much as Sydney loves hers."

"Here's to the ladies of Sycamore Way," they both say as we hold our glasses up in a toast.

The food is delicious. I place my hands on my full belly. This week, the baby hasn't been moving around as much. I read this is normal. He's probably a little cramped in there by now. Only a month and a half to go. Sydney holds up her corn on the cob covered hands, and Ali scoots her inside to wash up. I look over at Gemma, who is happily sipping her wine. She looks back at me.

"I know what you're thinking. And yeah, I do. One day," she says. "Have kids, I mean."

"You would have us all beat as mother of the year," I say. "You have a natural instinct to care for others."

"Thank you. You know, people ask me all the time why I don't have kids. It's the children's author slash love to cook and bake vibe. After I moved back to take care of my dad, I went on a lot of casual dates. It was more to pass the time than to find 'the one.' And then I guess I got comfortable being alone."

A bit of sadness lingers in the air before Gemma perks up again and says, "Dessert?" as Ali and Sydney come back out.

Ali says, "I don't know about you two, but I need to rest and digest before I eat more. And that might not be until tomorrow."

Sydney, full of energy as always, dances around the backyard with her polar bear, swinging it by both arms. Gemma heads in to retrieve a tray of desserts. Sydney stops twirling and turns to me.

"Auntie Victoria?" Sydney asks. "Is the baby awake?"

"Mm, I don't know. He's not moving right now," I tell her. "But his little foot is poking me. Here, give me your hand."

She giggles. I place her little hand on my belly and look up at Ali, who smiles.

"Gentle now, Syd," Ali says.

"I will, Mama," Sydney says, her words coming out in a whisper. Her little hand is right over the baby's foot, and I move it in a small circle over the area. Suddenly, the baby kicks, and a large ripple appears across my belly. Sydney jumps back and puts her hands over her mouth in surprise, giggling.

"Did you see that, Mama? He's in there. He's moving," she says, as she points to the exact spot on my belly where he kicked her.

"I saw. That's what you were like when you were in my belly," Ali says.

"Can I try again?" Sydney asks, giving me her hands.

Gently, I place both of her hands on my belly. My baby boy pushes against me, connecting with her touch. It's as if he knows she's there and is saying hello.

# Chapter 23



Spending time with Ali and her family makes me realize how desperate I am to have a normal life. Family, friends, food, fun, and laughter are all I need. I'm grateful for Emilio. He gave me the courage to walk away from my abusive relationship with Jack. It wasn't an easy decision. I know Emilio hopes we can have a real relationship one day, but to be honest, I can't see that ever happening. I'm not physically attracted to him at all. I'm sure he'll be a wonderful husband someday. Just not to me. He's more like a brother to me. I trust him and know he has my best interests at heart.

That's why my guilt is in overdrive as I give in to the urge to talk to my best friend. Picking up the phone, I call Scarlett, dialing *68 first to block my number. It should be fine. Just a quick check-in so she knows I'm safe. Her cell rings a few times before her voicemail kicks in. No luck. I hang up and switch over to one of my social media accounts instead. My profile is named *'browneyedgirl.'* It's what my grandpa used to call me. It's the only nickname I've ever had. I don't follow anyone, and I don't post anything, like Emilio and I agreed. I can only see public accounts. Luckily, both Scarlett's and Jack's accounts are set to public. I click onto Scarlett's account and see that she hasn't posted recently. The last photo was one of her at the hospital in her nurse's uniform. In it, she's smiling with a co-worker named Nancy. The caption says, "Twelve-hour day with this lovely lady. Time to go home!"

This takes me back to a memory of the time Scarlett and I worked back-to-back shifts because the hospital was short of nurses during COVID. Several of the nurses had gotten sick and were out of commission. The remaining nurses Door Dashed Taco Bell tacos, bean burritos, and power bowls to the hospital to keep us fueled. Scarlett was obsessed with the Baja Blast, so she ordered a ton of those as well. I wouldn't touch one of those with a ten-foot pole if you ask me. They're way too sweet.

"Hey, so when are you and Jack having kids?" she asks me.

"I don't know. When we're financially stable."

"Don't you have that trust that your grandparents left you? Isn't it like a quarter of a million dollars?"

"Yeah, but that's my emergency fund. And shhh, I told you, no one is supposed to know about that account except you."

"Not even Jack?" Scarlett asks, and I shake my head. "But he's your husband."

"Jack said we can start trying next year," I say.

"Really?" Scarlett says, reaching to hug me. "Oh, Care Bear! I'm so excited for you. I'll be the best auntie ever. I can't wait."

She took a sip of her Baja Blast.

"Do you think it will be a boy or a girl? Because if it's a girl, I think you should name her after me."

I laugh. "Well, you know, Jack would have a say in it too since he would be the daddy."

"Okay, but try to convince him. Scarlett Livingston. That's sexy."

I roll my eyes. "Did you call my baby sexy? You are such a ho, Scar."

"But I'm *your* ho," she says, putting her drink down. "Well, I need to go give Mr. Cassidy his enema. Ta ta!"

I laugh at the memory and am brought back to the present by my phone ringing. It's Scarlett. I guess *68 doesn't work after all.

"Hey, girl," I say, excited to hear my best friend's voice again.

"Care Bear, hey. Are you okay? Is this your new number?" she asks.

"Yeah, it is. How's everything back home? I miss you so much."

"Same, same, you know, work and stuff. Where are you? Are you coming back home?"

The question makes my heart plummet.

"Uh, Scar. I can't come back home. And I can't risk Jack finding me. I'm safe, though. Maybe we can FaceTime soon. I miss you so much."

"I would love that. I miss you too. Everyone at the hospital has been asking about you. I tell them that I don't know where you went, which is true," she says. "It's probably better that I don't know too much."

"Scar, I don't know how I'll raise this baby without you. It's been you and me since we were kids."

"Wait, did you have the baby already?" She says, her voice excited.

"No, not yet. This little guy is running out of room, though."

I'm about to tell her about Sydney and the other night, but then I think twice. She can't know about what goes on in Laurelville.

"Oh wow. I can't believe you'll be a mom soon. I wish I could be there when you give birth, Cara. Why can't you come back and divorce Jack?"

"I wish you could be here too, but you know how it is. Jack was getting worse as the days went on. The abuse was unbearable. I can't risk my safety. Or my baby's safety."

A very long, uncomfortable silence follows. I can hear shuffling in the background, and then a door slams.

"Have you seen Jack around town?" I ask her. There's no answer, no sound at all. It's like I've been muted.

"Scar? Are you there?"

Silence. I look at my phone, and it says I'm on a live call, the timer ticking. I put the phone back to my ear.

"Sorry. My foot got stuck in the blanket, and I dropped the phone. What was it you asked?"

"Jack. Have you seen or heard from him?"

"Uh, no," she says.

I can tell she's hiding something from me. Her tone has changed, and her answers are stiff. Before I can ask her about it, she says, "Hey, can you hold on a sec?"

"Yeah, sure," I tell her.

I hear more shuffling in the background and mumbling. I hear a door slam again, and Scarlett is back on the line.

"Sorry about that. Umm, I saw Jack a few weeks ago at the Valencia," she tells me. "He was with two guys from the shop."

"Did he say anything to you?"

"No, I left when I saw him."

"Is he looking for me? Have you heard anything?"

"What? No, I don't know. When you first left, he had all his mechanic friends looking for you. They showed up at my place thinking you were here."

"What did you tell them?"

"Nothing. Because I didn't know anything. I'm sure Jack is over you by now. It's been what? Over three months?"

"Something like that."

"So, how's Tony?"

I stop dead in my tracks. A gush rushes from between my legs. Did my water break? I hold my belly and look down at the puddle beneath me. The pungent smell of urine reaches my nose, and I realize I peed myself. I never told Scarlett I was with Tony.

"Cara? Are you there?" she says. "Hello?"

"What are you talking about, Scar? Why would you think I'm with Tony?"

"Cara, everyone knows you and Tony ran off together. It couldn't have been a coincidence that he disappeared, and then suddenly you were gone too. People aren't stupid. Maybe if you weren't pregnant, it would be more believable that you ran away on your own."

"Scar, I *am* by myself," I say. I grab a spray bottle of cleaner and a towel from the linen closet to clean the floor. "Tony moved months before I left. I think he relocated somewhere in the East Bay."

"And who's Emilio?" she asks.

I'm confused for a second. How does she know Emilio's name?

"What do you mean?"

"Your caller ID says Emilio Caruso. Who is that?"

*Shit.* I try to quickly come up with an explanation. I've never been a good liar.

"Emilio was the guy who I bought this phone from," I lie. "Don't tell anyone I called, okay? Especially Jack."

"Of course not," Scarlett says. "Hey, I've got to get ready for work. Talk to you later?"

"Yeah. Yeah, sure."

Then I hear it. A loud rumbling sound in the background. The line goes dead.

***

I'm pacing back and forth in the living room when Emilio comes home from work. I'm sick to my stomach, and not from the pregnancy. Emilio rushes over to me.

"What happened? Are you hurt?"

"Emilio, you're going to kill me. You were right. We need to leave. Now."

He observes our suitcases by the door.

"Slow down," he says. "Tell me from the beginning."

"I called Scarlett," I tell him. "I know you said not to. I'm so, so sorry. Please don't be mad."

The look on his face is one I have never experienced before. It's a cross between rage and fear. This gentle man has never raised his voice or a hand at me, but as I watch him walk into the kitchen, I know I've crossed the line. He plants his hands on the counter and breathes heavily. I've never seen him panic. He's always so calm and collected.

"I told you," he says, his voice hoarse.

"I know. I know you did. And I didn't listen," I tell him. "She's my best friend."

"She also has feelings for Jack," Emilio says. He slams his fist down on the counter. I've never seen him angry before. "Dammit, Victoria. I'm trying to protect you. If Jack finds out you're here. Hell, if Jack finds out I'm here, he'll kill us both. I told you there were rules. Did you think I made them up for no reason?"

"What do you mean she also has feelings for him?"

A look of frustration passes over Emilio's face.

"Didn't you notice anytime we went out, she would do little gestures like touch him on the arm or the hand? She would also say his name in a very sexy, flirty way. That drove me nuts. I know she's your friend, but she was so fake. She was very manipulative. It was Jack this or Jack that. Or laugh at things he said that weren't even funny."

He was right. She did that. A lot. I thought it was Scarlett being Scarlett. Since high school, she had earned a reputation for being slutty. In our college years, she was out of control with the number of guys she hooked up with. She even hooked up with a married teacher. It was part of her personality, and I ignored it because she was always a reliable and loyal friend to me. Never once did I suspect her of stealing any of the guys I was with. But Emilio had a point. She acted overly flirtatious with Jack. I didn't think anything of it because she did it right in front of me. Plus, she was my best friend. She wouldn't do that to me. Not after she saw how Jack treated me. *Would she?*

"Victoria, we need to change our numbers. Otherwise, Scarlett might trace where we are."

I hand Emilio my phone. He removes the SIM card and destroys it. Taking his phone out, he repeats the process.

"What did you tell Scarlett?" Emilio asks me, his voice calmer than before.

"Nothing. She asked where I was, and I told her I couldn't say. Then she asked how you were, and I told her that I didn't know. You and I are not together. That you moved to the East Bay long before I left Jack."

Emilio shakes his head. "What else?"

"She asked who Emilio Caruso was because of the caller ID. I made up something about how it was the person I bought the phone from."

"No, Victoria! We're in so much deep shit. Why didn't you block the caller ID? Scarlett will put two and two together that Emilio is my new name. And it's only a matter of time before she finds out your new name and where we are. Did you tell her anything else?"

"No, but I asked her if she had seen Jack. And I did try to block the caller ID. I typed *68 before I dialed."

Emilio shakes his head. "It's *67 to block the call. That's why it didn't work."

"Oh," I say sheepishly.

"What did she say about Jack?"

"She said she saw him at some club but didn't talk to him."

"That's it?"

I hesitate for a second. Emilio notices.

"Victoria, we promised not to keep things from one another. Whatever it is, you can tell me."

Although I didn't want to say anything about it, I knew I had to.

"At the end of our conversation, I heard his car. I'd know that sound anywhere," I tell him, because I know this time it really was Jack's car and not some delivery truck.

# Chapter 24

KEITH

I roll out of bed and grab my phone off the nightstand. Two voicemails and one text message. The first voicemail is from an older woman two blocks over who needs her garbage disposal looked at. The second one is from a man asking if I work on cars. The text message is from Gemma: Good morning! Come over for coffee if you're not too busy. I made scones too. Gemma's text makes me smile as I shower and get ready for the day.

So far, my homemade flyer has brought me several jobs on Sycamore Way and the surrounding streets. One of today's jobs is to program Ali and Brooks' fancy new refrigerator. I stop by Gemma's house to say hello to her and Chester. Her gorgeous face brings a smile to mine. It's the perfect beginning to a new day. As she hands me a cup of coffee and a little bag of scones, I lean down to kiss her. Her lips linger on mine and break into a smile as we pull apart. I'm sure I'm grinning like an idiot as well. We agreed to take things slow. I love spending time with Gemma. And Chester. Although I agreed to stick around to help Fiona fix up the house and be her neighborhood watchdog, part of me thinks I might want to extend my stay. As I head over to Ali and Brooks' house, the neighborhood is quiet, and I do a quick recon of all the houses on the block. Everything seems in place.

Ali answers the door with a smile on her face and waves me in.

"Thank you so much for doing this, Keith. Brooks wanted this top-of-the-line clunker, and I have no idea how to use it. There are so many buttons," Ali says.

"No problem. Here, let me test a few things, and then I'll show you how it works. We can go through the manual if you'd like, so that you know what's what. You'll be a pro in no time," I tell her.

"I don't know about that. Sydney will probably figure out how to use it before I do," Ali laughs.

I spend the next two hours at Ali and Brooks' house, programming their new refrigerator. I walk her through the controls and answer every question she throws at me.

"Call me if you need any help," I tell her.

"It sure is convenient having you right across the street," she says. She takes out a few bills and hands them to me. "I'm sure I'll be calling you again soon. Thanks again, Keith."

We make eye contact as I'm about to leave. *Is that a glimmer of recognition I see in your eyes, Ali?* It's been over seven years since I've seen her. Part of me is surprised she doesn't recognize me.

# Chapter 25

Victoria

"Okay, seriously, this is the cutest backyard," Ali says as she pushes aside the overgrown brush. "All it needs is a little tender loving care. Do you guys have a gardener?"

I tell her about the referral that Fiona gave us when we moved in. Neither Emilio nor I have called yet, which is why the plants and bushes are so overgrown. *I didn't know weeds could grow that quickly.*

"Oh, call him. His name is Johnson, and not only is he a gardener, but he has degrees in horticulture and landscaping. He will turn your yard into a magical wonderland."

"Really?" I ask, impressed.

"Yes, legit degrees. I forget what school he went to, but Johnson is extremely knowledgeable when it comes to foliage."

I make a mental note to call this Johnson guy. I don't have much time to get organized before the baby comes.

Gemma and Ali suggest a few decorating ideas for the inside and outside of my house. I love their enthusiasm. If it weren't for them, I would have no idea where to begin.

I lead them into the baby's room and watch as the wheels in their heads turn.

"Do you like it?" Ali asks me. "I mean, do you want to keep the cloud and airplane motif or change it up?"

"Yeah, I think I do like it. It's perfect for a little boy," I tell her. "Once he's older, we can always change it to what he likes."

She nods and opens the dresser drawer.

"Looks like you need a little bit of everything," Ali says as she peeks into the almost empty drawers. She takes the Bible out and opens it. "Hmm, this is the same Bible that Fiona left me for Sydney, only mine reads, 'to my dear little girl.' It's like she thinks all the kids on Sycamore are hers."

"Well, that's creepy. But that's Fiona for you," Gemma says. "Hey, do you think she did the same thing for Seamus and Darby when they moved here? Ramona was only a baby."

Ali shrugs. "I guess I never thought about it. We should ask Darby. I'm sure Fiona was their realtor also."

Ali and Gemma measure and brainstorm more. They remind me of mad scientists on a mission to create the perfect potion. It makes me smile to see how happy they are to help me. When they're done, we agree to meet in half an hour for lunch and shopping in Locke City.

***

"Hey, how cute is this?" Ali asks. She holds up a giant stuffed bear and gives it a huge squeeze.

I laugh. "No, way. That thing is bigger than the baby's bedroom."

She laughs and then puts it back down. "I guess I see what you're saying. It's so cute and cuddly, though."

Ali, Gemma, and I walk through the baby store, oohing and ahhing over all the cute baby items. I decide on a few items that will make my life easier once the baby arrives, such as a baby wipe warmer and a set of baby bottles. I'm beginning at ground zero, so I need almost everything. Gemma puts a case of size two diapers in the cart.

"Let's buy a few necessities today. Ali and I have a surprise for you," Gemma says, a twinkle in her eye.

It takes me a minute before I realize the surprise must be a baby shower.

"No! You didn't. You don't have to do anything like that," I tell them.

"Like what? I didn't tell you what the surprise is," Gemma says, a mischievous glimmer in her eye. She takes my hands in hers and says, "I'm so excited for you. Thank you for letting me and Ali help you."

"I should be thanking you," I say, then, "I've never had real girlfriends growing up. This is so generous of you both."

We grab a few more adorable baby items. I choose a jungle animal print onesie and a two-pack of fleece footie pajamas. All this walking around has caused the baby to shift around.

After paying at the front register, I need to pee quite urgently. The baby is pressing on my bladder. Ali and Gemma wait for me at the front of the store as I hurry to the back to use the restroom. I enter the first stall and lock the door behind me. I almost don't make it to the toilet. As I finish, the bathroom door opens, and someone enters. I can see the shadow of the person's legs. Whoever it is moves from one stall to the next. Mine first, then the doors of the two empty stalls next to me swing open. A lump forms in my throat. Why push open both empty stalls? Obviously, it's not Gemma or Ali because either would acknowledge me.

The shadow travels back to my stall and stops. I hold my breath. The person shuffles to the sink area and turns the water on. I'm sure I'm being silly. Jack won't find me in the women's restroom of BabyMart. I think about texting Gemma, but realize I don't have a phone right now. My heart pounds, and I take a deep breath. I flush the toilet and slowly move to unlock the door. I pray the person leaves before me. The stall door creaks open, grazing my pregnant belly. I'm staring at the back of someone I know all too well. Scarlett.

Panic washes over me, followed by a sense of uneasiness. I do a double-take. Am I imagining her? She turns and reaches out to hug me, then puts her hands on my belly.

"Scar. Why are you here?" I ask her.

"What? No, hi, best friend, I'm so happy to see you," Scarlett says. "You're about to pop! I can't believe I found you."

"I...I..." I am at a loss for words. I haven't seen Scarlett in over three months.

"You can't be here," I whisper to Scarlett, although there is no one else in the restroom besides us. "How did you find me?"

Her face changes as if she remembers why she's here. She takes my hands in hers.

"Cara, I'm here to warn you that Jack found out where you're at. I lied the last time we talked. He is super obsessed with finding you. He saw the area code you called me from and went ballistic. He's pissed you're with that Emilio guy and wants to know who he is. He doesn't have your address, though. At least, I don't think he does. He only knows it's in this town. I figured you'd have to go to the store eventually, so I've been in the parking lot all day. What is this town anyway, Care Bear? It's like Hicksville. They don't even have a Starbucks."

"Why would you tell him I called, Scar?"

"I didn't tell him. After you left him, Jack was beside himself. We hung out a few times. When he came over the other day to pick up a tool he left at my place, he saw the call on my phone and asked me who Emilio was. I told him it was a wrong number. When he saw the number came from this town, he went nuts. I'm not sure how he connected it to you, but somehow he knew."

"What the hell, Scarlett? You think I believe that story? You're supposed to be my best friend. After everything he did to me, the least you could do is keep your mouth shut."

"It's the truth, Cara. Jack was so depressed afterward. He needed a friend."

"So what? You decided you would be the one to comfort him? My abusive, almost-ex-husband? Did you sleep with him?"

Her silence was enough of an answer to make me run back to the toilet and vomit. After what Scarlett and I have been through, you would think her loyalty would lie with me. I stand up and go back over to the sink to rinse my mouth and wash my hands. Scarlett's eyes are rimmed red.

"I'm sorry Cara. It happened only once. He was so upset. And why would you care anyway? You don't even want to be with him anymore. You're with this Emilio guy. Tell me how you pulled that one off. Is he one of those guys who is obsessed with pregnant women?"

I'm so mad I could hit her. "No. I told you. I bought the phone from Emilio so it wouldn't be in my name. Even though I'm not with Jack anymore, it doesn't mean you can have my sloppy seconds. Maybe I was blind all these years. Maybe you really are the slut everyone makes you out to be. So, where is he? Did you lead him right to me?"

Scarlett stares at me in disbelief. I know what I said was harsh, but of all the men she could sleep with, she chose Jack. *Why would you stab me in the back like that, Scarlett? What did I ever do to you?*

"What? No. As soon as he told me the name of this city, I hopped on a plane and flew down here to warn you. I didn't tell him I'm here. You're my best friend, Cara. More than that, you're like a sister to me. You have to believe that."

I want to believe Scarlett, but there's no way I can trust her.

"There's one more thing," Scarlett says.

*How could this situation get any worse?*

"Jack knows about the money from your grandparents."

"What? How did he find out?"

Her brow furrows. "I didn't realize you were still keeping that a secret from him. I'm sorry."

"Wow, so not only did you screw my abusive ex, then lead him straight to me, but you also told him about my secret emergency fund? The one I told you he didn't know about? That one, Scar? You know what, Scarlett? You can fuck off. I don't ever want to speak to you or Jack again," I push past her.

I meet Ali and Gemma at the front of the store, my face red, my breath shallow. It takes me a minute to get my bearings.

"Are you okay?" Ali asks. "You don't look well."

"I'm fine. It's nothing. I had a few Braxton-Hicks contractions while I was in the ladies' room. Let's go, please," I say, close to tears. I don't dare turn around to see where Scarlett has gone.

# Chapter 26



By the time we arrive back on Sycamore Way, I have little to no energy left in me. The bond I've accrued with Ali and Gemma is so unexpected. I'm not accustomed to girlfriends who don't look at me like a vagabond. I'm grateful for their generosity and for welcoming me with open arms. All my life, I've kept people at arm's length so that I wouldn't get hurt. I focused so much on school and work that I didn't exactly have time for a social life. Scarlett and I became friends out of necessity, but then our relationship grew. We were like sisters—Scarlett, the older sibling, and me, the one she protected. No matter what, though, we always had each other's backs. As I think back on the dynamics of our relationship, I wonder, *did she always think I was beneath her? Did I misread her intentions from day one? Is that what she thought of me? And did she have her eye on Jack while I was with him, like Emilio said?* All I know is that after today, she's no longer my best friend. I can no longer trust her.

As we unload Ali's SUV, there's a pop in my lower back, and I feel achy. Another yawn escapes. *Did I catch a cold, or is it from the stress?* My eyes don't want to stay open.

"You should take a nap," Ali says. "When I was pregnant with Sydney, all I wanted to do was sleep."

"Even the smallest tasks use up so much energy," I tell her, relieved that she understands.

Gemma and Ali ask if I need anything. I wish I could tell them what happened back at the store, but I know that I need to err on the side of caution. Even though they're my new friends, I don't want to scare either of them off with my drama.

After I head into the house to rest my weary feet, I take my shoes off and groan when I see the side of my feet and ankles. They're humongous. Propping them up on a pillow, a deep exhale escapes my lips as I'm guided into a deep slumber.

The sound of a dog barking pulls me back to the land of the living. I reach for my phone, then realize I don't have one anymore. Emilio and I tossed the burner phones after he purchased the smartphones for us. He said he would pick up new SIM cards and change our numbers after work today. Emilio made me promise not to call Scarlett again. Not that it matters now. I don't ever want to speak to her again. I shake the cobwebs from my head and recall my conversation with Scarlett. It won't be long before Jack finds us in this small town. I need to warn Emilio.

After I empty my bladder, I head to the kitchen. Should I go to Gemma's and use her phone to call Emilio at work? The clock reads 5:00 p.m. Shoot. It's too late. Emilio is on his way home by now.

I head to the refrigerator for a bottle of water, but a shiny object on the counter catches my attention. My eyes are still a bit fuzzy from falling asleep with my contact lenses. As I come closer to the object, I see it's my phone. There's a small slip of paper underneath it. The note reads:

**V-**

**I got us new SIM cards and registered the phones under your name instead of mine. Don't make the same mistake again. Scarlett can't be trusted.**

**-E**

Emilio must have come home while I was asleep. I look around for any sign of him and call out, but there's no answer. The Chevy is parked in the driveway, so he must be here. Or maybe he went over to Gemma's to assist her with a task. My eyes stop on the key rack, where a single car key hangs next to my set of house keys. *Why did Emilio leave the car keys but keep his house keys?* Something isn't right.

I power my cell phone on. Emilio has programmed his new number into it as well as numbers for Gemma, Ali, and Fiona. I don't dare add Scarlett's number, which I have memorized, for fear that I'll give in and call her. I send Emilio a text: Where are you? Thanks for the new SIM card. I promise I won't mess up this time. Please call me.

The baby is like a bowling ball that weighs me down, so I hightail it to the couch, where I look through my phone. It's logged into a new Apple ID account: EVC251. Emilio Victoria Caruso, plus our address. That's easy to remember. Are both phones logged into the same account? I check the Notes app. It doesn't appear that Emilio and I are on the same Apple ID, although there's a shared note with the login for our Apple ID, as well as some other logins and passwords. I check my messages again. He still hasn't answered me. I text Gemma: Hey, it's Victoria. This is my new number. Have you heard from Emilio?

The three dots appear, and Gemma's response comes through.

No, I haven't seen him. I'm over at Ali's if you want to come hang out.

I call Emilio's phone. It rings seven times before sending me to a voicemail box with a generic message. I sit and stare into space and think of all the scenarios. Not one makes sense where he leaves the car key here, though. Unless he's not planning to come back and has left me the car. *He wouldn't do that, right?*

A knock at the front door pulls me out of my spiral of negative thoughts. I place my hand over my heart and take a deep breath. *Get a grip, Victoria.*

I put my eye to the peephole. Gemma and Chester are on the porch.

"Oh, hey. Sorry. I was about to text you back," I tell her.

"Did you find Emilio?" she asks as I move aside to let her and Chester in.

"No, I've texted and called. No answer."

"Well, the car is in the driveway, so he couldn't have gone far, right?"

"Right," I tell her. "He left the keys to the car here, but his house keys are gone."

The expression on Gemma's face when she's stumped is a cross between Scooby Doo and the Mad Hatter, and I'd laugh if I weren't so worried about Emilio's sudden disappearance. Finally, she says, "It's almost 6:00 p.m.. Let's take a walk and ask around. Chester and I will come with you."

Gemma, Chester, and I walk the neighborhood and knock on doors, but no one has heard from Emilio. I can tell that although Gemma is trying to comfort me, she's as worried as I am. As we walk, I am prepared to dart into the nearest bush at any sign of Jack. I keep my eyes and ears peeled.

"How about you come stay at my place tonight? We can hang out and do girl stuff. You can leave Emilio a note," Gemma says.

I weigh the pros and cons of staying at Gemma's house. It would help take my mind off Emilio's disappearance and make me feel safer now that Jack might find me at any minute. I don't want to be alone at a time like this. But how did Jack link the phone number to me if Scarlett didn't tell him? She must have told him. I grab my large tote and pack it with a few belongings, as well as my cash and the stuffed polar bear Gemma gave us.

# Chapter 27

Gemma

The shriek of sirens and shouting outside jolts me awake. Chester's frantic barks echo through the house. The thunderous pounding on the front door rattles the floorboards beneath me, and for a moment, I cling to the hope that this is only a nightmare. But through the windows, a hungry blaze surges closer. Heart racing, I stumble into the living room and throw the front door open, Chester by my side.

"Ma'am, we need to get you out of here. Is there anyone else in the house?" a firefighter in full gear asks me.

I almost say no, but then I remember Victoria is staying in my guest bedroom. I run to the room and turn the door handle. It's locked. I call out Victoria's name, and she rushes to the door.

"Gemma! What's happening?" she asks as she rubs the sleep from her eyes.

Then she sees it. The blaze is coming from next door. From her house. The firefighter ushers us out. Victoria yells, "Wait!" and runs into the room to grab her tote bag. I snatch my purse and Chester's leash from the entryway table.

By now, the entire neighborhood has spilled onto the street, the crowd gathered beneath the glow of flashing red lights as firefighters unleash torrents of water onto Victoria's burning house. Smoke curls upward, and Victoria and I make our way toward Ali's house, eager to escape the sting that burns our throats and eyes. She clutches her tote bag tight against her side, her wide, stunned eyes fixed on the inferno that consumes her home. Then my gaze shifts, and it lands on Fiona at the edge of the crowd. She's silent, observing.

The fire is extinguished within the hour, although the billows of smoke linger in the air. I ask a firefighter what the next steps are. He says they'll make sure the fire is entirely suppressed before they search for the cause of the fire. In the meantime, everyone on the block is safe and can go back inside. Poor Victoria. I can't believe this. The worst part of it is that Emilio is still missing. I can't help but wonder if he was in the house when it caught fire. I hope he wasn't.

# Chapter 28



I lie here awake, watching videos on TikTok, mainly of service dogs and their people. After spending time with Chester, I miss owning a dog. My ex-girlfriend wasn't a fan of pets of any kind. That should have been my first sign to get out of the relationship. I stand and peek out the window. The fire sure was a big one. I'm sure the neighbors are all spooked by now. We're lucky the first responders in this small town have a quick response time. Otherwise, the entire neighborhood would have burned to ashes. A series of loud bangs on my front door interrupts my thoughts. *Who the hell is that?*

I grab the gun out of my nightstand and double-check the magazine. Loaded and ready. The banging continues, and I yell out, "Okay, okay, I'm coming."

It's Fiona, of course. Sliding the safety back into place, I slide the gun into the waist of my jeans.

"Hello, Fiona. Do you know what time it is?" I ask, feigning sleepiness.

The crease between her eyebrows tells me it's not the time to fuck with her, so I shut up and cut the act. I'm in for a razzing, so I walk into the kitchen to make a pot of coffee. It'll be a long day.

"We have a problem."

I take a deep breath.

"Have you seen or heard anything?" she asks.

"Other than that massive fire?" I chid. "Nope."

Fiona taps her fingers on the kitchen counter.

"Look, I've only been here a few weeks. I've helped a few neighbors here and there. Everything is in place as far as I can tell."

"You've been keeping an eye on Victoria?"

"Yes, I've done as you've requested. The women of Sycamore have taken well to her."

"I noticed that too. That's good. It's an added layer of protection."

"Yes, ma'am. It is."

"Gemma said Victoria hasn't been able to locate Emilio."

"Since when?"

"Since this morning."

"Did he go to work?"

"I'll have to call Sal at the bakery to find out. In the meantime, you keep careful watch over that young lady. I want nothing to happen to her. And tell me if Emilio contacts you."

"Do you think Jack's found her?"

"I'm not sure. Victoria's burner phone didn't show any calls were made. You haven't noticed anyone snooping around in the neighborhood? A woman, maybe?"

I shake my head. I have no clue what she's talking about.

# Chapter 29



Gemma flips pancakes as I pace back and forth in her kitchen until she tells me to sit down. I'm making her nervous. Although my coffee is decaf, I'm jittery and can't keep still. *What did the police find? Do they have information on who burned my house down? Was it Jack?* My fingers are itching to call Scarlett to see if she knows more about Jack's whereabouts, but I know that would be stupid. She's probably back home in the Bay Area by now.

Emilio is still not answering his phone. My mind races with the possibilities of what could have happened. *Did Jack kidnap Emilio? If so, why did Emilio leave me the car key? He must have known he wouldn't be back last night. Did Jack follow Scarlett here and then run into Emilio?* Gemma suggests checking the Find My Friends app to see if I can locate Emilio's phone, but his phone is not connected to my app.

'Laurelville Police Department' pops up on my caller ID. My stomach clenches into a knot as I answer. "Hello?"

"Hello, Mrs. Caruso?" the voice on the other end says.

"Yes, this is she."

"This is Officer Bruce of the Laurelville Police Department. Are you available to come down to the station? We have some information we'd like you to see."

"Umm, sure. Now?"

"Yes, ma'am. It will only take a few minutes."

"Okay, I think my neighbor can take me."

"See you soon."

***

"Thank you again, Gemma. I'm so sorry to put you out." I feel bad about interrupting Gemma while she's working on her new book. But as always, she's in a calm and pleasant mood. I would have driven myself in the Chevy, which ironically survived the fire, but with my huge belly, it wouldn't have been comfortable at all. Sitting in the car as a passenger makes my sides hurt from the extra weight.

"Don't be silly. You're doing nothing of the sort. This is a traumatic experience. I'm happy to help. Plus, I need a break from my book today. I can't get my illustration of the little black kitten pawing at a ball of yarn right."

Gemma and I enter the police station, where I ask for Officer Bruce at the front desk. I'm seated in a small room with a metal table and two metal chairs that are bolted to the ground. The mirror that is mounted to one wall is exactly like the double-sided ones they show on TV. I wonder who, if anyone, is on the other side of it.

"Thank you for coming in on such short notice, Mrs. Caruso," Officer Bruce says as he places a file folder on the table in front of me. The officer sits in the chair opposite and opens the file. He lays out a few photos of the charred furniture and some of our personal belongings. I stare at the picture of the airplane mobile covered in soot, and sadness washes over me. *Who am I kidding? We never had a chance at being a normal family. Bad luck follows me wherever I go.*

I shake the pity-party thoughts from my head. I need to be strong for my little boy. Officer Bruce waits for me to look through the ten to twelve photos, then says, "Now, Mrs. Caruso, I'm warning you. These next photos are quite graphic. They were taken in the basement of your house."

I nod. *Why are they graphic? What was in the basement?* Officer Bruce places four glossy photographs in front of me, and it takes me a few seconds to understand what I'm looking at. The photos show a charred skeleton, reminiscent of the plastic toy ones you would find at a Halloween store. I hold the images closer to the light. Those are real bones.

"What? Who?" I ask, my voice quivering. I can't get the words out.

"We found human remains in your basement—what looks like a full skeleton, along with a few other bone fragments several feet away. The bones are badly charred. Mrs. Caruso, do you have any idea who this could be?"

A loud gurgle erupts from my stomach. I race to the small garbage can in the corner of the room in time to vomit up my lunch. I take several deep breaths, then lift my head. Officer Bruce holds out a package of wet wipes.

"Thank you," I say, plucking one from the package.

"Take your time. I understand this must be a shock."

And then I tell him. "I'm not sure. We moved in recently, and my husband is missing. Do you think it could be him?"

The officer helps me stand and slowly guides me back to the table and chair. The anxiety in the pit of my belly claws at my insides, and I clench my fists to stop the tears. I inhale a few deep breaths, and the officer slides over a bottle of water. I open it and take a few sips. He's watching me carefully. *Do the police think I could have burned the house down and killed this person in the basement? Am I a suspect?* I look into the officer's eyes but can't get a read on him.

"We won't confirm who the body belongs to until forensics is finished with it, so let's not panic or assume for now. We'd like to get a DNA sample of your husband to match it against. I'll have an officer contact you regarding your husband's disappearance."

My nurse's brain analyzes the skeleton to see if I can distinguish whether the body is male or female. A female's pelvis is typically wider and shorter because they give birth. I can't find a clear photo of that area of the body, though. Too bad I don't have a magnifying glass to zoom in on the image. I squint my eyes to focus better. *What's that speck of red in the basement's corner? A spot on the photo after it was developed, or a reflection of light off a piece of debris?*

"Notice anything?" the officer asks.

I shake my head.

"The firefighters believe the fire originated in the basement with an accelerant. Gasoline, maybe kerosene? We found empty cans in your backyard. Do you recall seeing them in the basement before the night of the fire?"

"No, um, I've never been in the basement of the house. We only moved in a little over a month ago. My friends and I went shopping yesterday so that we could..." And then I realize, I no longer have a house to decorate. My life has done a complete three-sixty. I'm back where I started from when I was a little girl with nowhere to go.

# Chapter 30



*Why would anyone want to burn down Victoria's house? Surely no one on Sycamore Way would be capable of this. We all have our secrets, but do Victoria and Emilio have the type of secrets that can get our house set on fire? Or worse, get someone killed?* These thoughts are why, after I return from a trip to the grocery store, I sit Victoria down. I need to know if she's in danger. Or if I am.

"I'm sorry, Gemma. You have every right to be concerned. First, Emilio disappears, and then we have a house fire." She pauses to see my reaction. I stay calm and ready to listen so she continues. "Emilio and I moved here to live a more secluded lifestyle. Away from any big cities. We never meant for any of this to happen."

Victoria tells me about her abusive, soon-to-be ex-husband, Jack. Since she and Emilio arrived in Laurelville, she's still on edge from the trauma she experienced. It all makes sense to me now, especially when she tells me that Keith looks a lot like Jack. That must be why she was acting so odd when I waved the day we were out for a walk.

"So, the baby?" I ask her.

"He's not Emilio's. If that's what you're asking. Emilio and I have a platonic relationship. He wants more, and I've told him many times that I love him, but not like that."

I take a minute to digest this material.

"Do you think your husband killed Emilio and set your house on fire to destroy the evidence?"

"That would make sense. I can't be sure, though," she says. "I don't know what to do. I'm about to have this baby, and I'm scared out of my mind. I sense Jack's energy around me everywhere I go."

I lean over and hug her. She quietly sobs into my shoulder, her shoulders shaking with each inhale. She leans back and wipes the tears away.

"I only wanted a normal life. I thought this was it. Everyone has been so generous and friendly. I want to fit in here. So badly."

"You do. We all love you. And Emilio," I wipe a tear from my cheek, sad for her and sad for Emilio. "You have to remember one thing."

"What's that?"

"They still haven't confirmed it's Emilio. We can't give up hope that he's out there. Maybe he's as scared as you are."

# Chapter 31

Victoria

Officer Bruce calls to tell me the formal police report from the fire is released and that I can come and pick up a copy at my earliest convenience. I'm eager to find out what the forensic pathologists found. *Did they discover who it was?* Gemma drives me down to the station, and we stop at the store to pick up a few items for lunch before heading back to her house. In the car, I read the report out loud.

"Incident number 51075. Description: Firefighters respond to a call of smoke seen exiting a structure on Sycamore Way on 8/10/23 at approximately 10:15 p.m. Upon arrival, firefighters observe flames extending from the windows at 251 Sycamore Way. The house, built in 1951, was purchased by Fiona C. Adams in 2014. The cause of the fire is arson with origination in the basement of the house; gasoline was used as the accelerant. Three empty gasoline containers were found in the backyard and are believed to have been used in the fire. No fingerprints were found on the containers. The fire left V-shaped markings on the remaining walls and fixtures. Firefighters contained and suppressed the fire within two hours of arrival and used cooling techniques from nearby hydrants. Residents of nearby houses were evacuated until the fire was suppressed. Furthermore, the body of a deceased female was found in the basement. The body has not been identified to date, as it was badly burned, and forensics could not extract a viable DNA sample. Police are creating a composite sketch of what the woman may have looked like when she was alive. Several feet from the body, another set of bones, which were almost completely decomposed, was discovered. These have yet to be identified. After further investigation, the cause of death for the female was a gunshot wound to the head. Burns were secondary. The body showed no signs of trauma other than the gunshot wound and fire. Time of death is inconclusive because of the state of the body. Firefighters approximate the fire was started between 9:30 p.m. and 10:00 p.m. Neighbors on Sycamore Way, including the occupant of the house, Victoria Caruso, were interviewed the day following the fire."

"It says the body was a female," I say.

"Who do you think it could be?" Gemma asks.

The color in my face drains. My mind immediately thinks back to my conversation with Scarlett. *Did Jack find out she came here to warn me? Did he kill her when he found out?* When

Jack was angry, he became another person. His anger and jealousy consumed him.

"What? Tell me what's going through that head of yours," Gemma demands.

I give in and tell her about Scarlett and our phone conversation. Then, I tell her about running into Scarlett at BabyMart.

"I'm sorry I didn't tell you," I say. "The last thing I said to her was to fuck off. What kind of best friend am I? The worst kind."

"She betrayed you by sleeping with your abusive husband. How else are you supposed to act? I'd be mad as hell."

"You're right. It's a punch to the gut. We went through so much together. She was the person I could trust when there wasn't anyone else. Until now, I mean."

Gemma gives me a minute to calm down. I take several deep breaths.

"So, do you think that means Jack is here too? Do you think that's why Emilio disappeared?"

"I'm not sure," I tell her. "Why would Jack want to kill Scarlett?"

"Maybe, he thought Scarlett betrayed him by coming to see you," Gemma says.

She has a point. I can't wrap my head around what's happened. *Does this mean Jack was in our house?*

"Does the police report list alibis?" she continues. "Where was everyone the night the fire happened?"

I turn to the third page of the report.

"No one really has an alibi other than Seamus and Darby, who were out of town and have hotel receipts to prove it. Freddy, Penelope, and the kids were already in bed. Keith and Fiona were each in their respective houses alone after a late dinner in Locke City at around 9:15 p.m. You and I were here. Ali and Sydney were home. Brooks was at his San Diego work apartment. None of this is useful. Everyone was where they usually are at night."

I hand the papers over to Gemma, who scans them once more.

"Oh, but what about this? When the police interviewed Freddy and Penelope's nanny, Helga, she stayed for dinner that night and left at around 8:00 p.m. She remembered an unfamiliar blue car driving down the street."

"Jack," I say, chills running down my spine. "But wasn't the fire much later than that?"

"Mm hmm. The fire was started between 9:30 p.m. and 10:00 p.m., but they don't have a timeframe for when the person was killed."

"Why didn't we hear a gunshot? The whole neighborhood would have heard it," I say. "And if Jack was in my house and left at 8:00 p.m., then did he come back and light the fire a couple of hours later?"

"I know nothing about guns," Gemma says. "So, I can't help you there. The timeline is a bit fuzzy, though. What I don't understand is what does Jack want?"

"Me. To hurt me. To punish me for running from him. And the money."

"The money?"

I tell Gemma about my trust fund and how Scarlett told Jack about it despite the fact that I told her not to.

"That's awful," she says.

"Maybe Emilio scared him off," Gemma suggests.

"But if that's the case, where's Emilio now?"

Neither Gemma nor I wanted to state the obvious. *Are Emilio and Jack working together? Did Emilio make a deal with Jack?* The thought of it leaves goosebumps on my skin.

Gemma taps her fingers on the table.

"Huh?" I ask.

"Do you think there's something odd about Keith and Fiona?"

I raise my brow. What is she talking about?

"Well, first they were out to dinner the night of the fire. Late. Why would Fiona and Keith be out to dinner? Then, Ali said she couldn't fall back asleep that night. Her adrenaline was pumping from watching your house go down in flames. If there's one thing I've observed about Ali over the years, it's that her intuition is spot on. It's as if she sees things before they happen. She told me two days ago that she felt like something was not right on Sycamore, but that she couldn't pinpoint exactly what was off. Anyway, she ended up reading a book in bed that night," Gemma says. "Ali's bedroom window faces out to the street."

"Did she see something out of the ordinary?"

Gemma nods. "She said Fiona went over to Keith's at 4:00 a.m. and didn't leave until at least 7:00 a.m."

# Chapter 32

Gemma

The next morning, Victoria surprises me by asking if I would go next door with her. Although the police caution tape is gone, most of the house is burnt to a crisp.

"Why would you want to do that?" I ask as I place the last deviled egg on the platter.

"I thought I saw something in the photos at the police station. It could be nothing, but I'd like to go check it out. I don't want to go alone, though."

We sneak in through the side gate, which is partially charred from the fire. The gate creaks loudly as we close it.

"Geez, I guess being stealthy is out of the question," she says.

"It makes you wonder how someone snuck back here without being heard."

The damp, soot-filled living room greets us upon entry. It feels as if the oxygen has been sucked out of the house. Victoria covers her face with her hand. Traipsing down the seventeen steps to the basement, the smell of smoke is exponentially worse and is mixed with the smell of chemicals.

"Maybe we shouldn't be down here. This air can't be good for the baby," I tell her, but she holds up a finger and says, "One sec."

Victoria hurries over to the corner and bends over, her baby bump stopping her mid-bend.

"Here, let me help you," I say.

Victoria points to a small object covered in soot. I pick it up and place it in my palm, and hold it out to her. She blows the soot off and rubs the piece of metal. The letter S appears. The heart-shaped locket reveals two tiny pictures, one on each side.

"It's Scarlett and me when we were in high school. We saved our money up to buy these. I have the matching necklace with the initial "C" on it.

"C?" I ask.

Victoria looks up and smiles, as if a happy memory has popped into her consciousness. "My real name is Cara."

It takes me a minute to realize what this means. Scarlett's necklace is down here because Scarlett was down here. Which means Victoria (or Cara) was right. The dead body belongs to Scarlett. Either that, or Scarlett was the killer. I have a feeling Victoria hasn't told me everything.

# Chapter 33

Victoria

Now that the police have identified the body as that of a female and not a male, they're treating Emilio's disappearance as a missing persons case. After they grill me about Emilio's family, friends, and acquaintances, the police give up. I have nothing. I gave them the cover story, which Emilio and I made up. We met in a bar in San Diego two years ago and got married on a drunken night in Vegas. When they asked for a copy of our marriage license, I told them we had misplaced our marriage license and never ordered another copy. I hope they don't follow through and try to obtain a copy because they won't find one. I told them I got pregnant last year, and we decided to move somewhere quiet to raise a family. After months of research, Emilio found Laurelville on the map and saw there were a few houses available for rent. He called the realtor, Fiona Adams, and the rest is history. The truth of the matter is, Emilio could be anywhere by now. What scares me is that Jack might hold him against his will. I wouldn't put it past him. Jack doesn't take betrayal lightly. I've seen the anger in his eyes when he thinks someone is trying to get one over on him. Emilio was one of his best friends. I wouldn't put it past Jack to torture Emilio and let him die a slow death.

As Gemma and I walk down to Keith's house to bring him some freshly baked bread, I casually mention I've been looking for a studio apartment to rent. I don't want to put her or anybody else in danger. Gemma lists all the reasons why I should continue to stay with her when we see Fiona coming out of her house, frantically waving at us.

"Victoria, I have been meaning to come and speak to you," Fiona says. She stops in front of us.

*Uh, oh. Is she mad at me because the house burned down?*

"Hi, Fiona. How are you? I've been meaning to come talk to you as well. I'm so sorry that..."

"No, no, don't worry about the house. That's what insurance is for. All my properties are fully insured for every disaster that could happen. I'm sorry you were only in it for such a short time. I was looking forward to seeing your son grow up in that house."

And then the oddest thing happens. She leans over to give me a hug. I must not be the only one who thinks it's strange because I hear Gemma stifle a laugh.

"Thank you, Fiona. I appreciate that."

"Anywho, although you are about to pop any minute now, I want to ask you if you have a plan for after the baby is born."

"Not really. My pregnancy brain is out of control right now. I'll need to figure out childcare and a job. Nowadays, I'm too tired to research anything. With Emilio not here, I feel out of sorts. He was my rock."

"Oh, dear. I understand. Have you heard anything more from the police? They haven't identified the body yet is what I hear."

"No, they haven't. It was a female, though, so it couldn't be Emilio. I don't understand why he won't answer his phone or why he would abandon us. It doesn't make sense. I want to search for him, but I have no idea where to look. I'm scared he might be in trouble."

"You've got that right. It makes no sense at all. Perhaps we could ask everyone on the street to keep an eye out for him."

"I'm so mentally and physically exhausted. All I want to do is sleep," I tell her.

"That's what I was hoping you'd say. Hear me out," Fiona says, as she touches my arm with her cherry-red manicured hand. "I was at the office the other day, running around, answering phones, scheduling meetings, and suddenly it hit me. The last time I had a front desk girl was over a year ago. After Lydia left, I never hired anyone else. The realtors in the office, there are five of us, ended up doing our own thing. It would be wonderful to have a person there to answer the phones and schedule appointments for us again. I thought it would be the perfect position for you. I mean, I don't know what you did back where you came from, but this type of work would be rather stress-free. Ideal for a new sleep-deprived mother. Would you be interested once you're ready to go back to work?"

I'm in shock. How is it possible that these people on Sycamore are so kind? I think I'm in the Twilight Zone. I manage to say the word "yes" when Gemma butts in.

"What about childcare?" Gemma asks.

A devilish smile spreads across the older woman's face, and she turns to me. "I've taken care of that as well. Provided it's okay with you, of course."

She explains that since Brodie and Oakley are in school full-time, Penelope doesn't need the nanny as much now as when they were little. Helga has been caring for the boys since they were toddlers and often babysits the other children on the block. Fiona tells me that she would be more than happy to pay Helga to watch my baby while I'm at work. The hours at her office would be part-time from 9:00 a.m. to 3:00 p.m. This is a dream come true. I accept the offer with a tear in my eye, and Fiona tells me, "Now, you focus on taking care of yourself and that little guy in there. We're not only friends here on Sycamore Way, we're family, too. You'll be okay. Oh, and I almost forgot."

Fiona holds out an envelope with my name on it.

"It's a check for the remainder of the rent you and Emilio paid, plus your security deposit. It's only fair since the house is now uninhabitable. I plan on rebuilding as soon as we can get the contractors lined up."

My heart gives a brief flutter. This extra money will surely come in handy. "Thank you," I say.

# Chapter 34



It's a relief to know that I have a future and some extra cash. Fiona's offer is more than generous, but a tiny part of me can't help but wonder why she's offering me this opportunity. *Can I trust her?* Where I'm from, it's everyone for themselves. *Maybe small towns are different in that respect.*

Despite Gemma's protests, I peruse the Internet to search for a small apartment nearby. I don't need a lot of space. I've had to get creative in my contributions to Gemma's household since she won't accept money from me. This means earning my keep in other ways. I have been cleaning her house from top to bottom and asking her for minor projects. It's mainly simple tasks such as organizing drawers and closets. These projects help me keep my hands busy and my mind sane. It's funny, but I find it therapeutic. Soothing music on Spotify puts me in a relaxed mood. However, sometimes I can't help my mind from drifting off to Emilio's whereabouts. I still can't believe he's gone. Whether he's dead, was kidnapped, or had to flee for some unknown reason, I guess I'll never know. It's already been two weeks since the fire. Even though I didn't love him like a boyfriend or husband, I loved him as a friend and a protector. I hope he knows how much I appreciate him.

Waddling over to the shed in Gemma's backyard, after she explains to me that while some people have a junk drawer in their house, she has a junk shed full of plastic tubs with random bits and pieces. I take my time to empty one tub at a time and laugh at some items in the bins. There's a wide variety—from a pair of pliers to batteries to a medal for a 5k in 1995. If there's one thing I'm sure of, it's that Gemma hates to run. I'll have to ask her about the 5K. As I work my way to the back of the shed, an object wedged between the wall of the shed and a tub reveals itself. There's a hole in the shed where the two walls meet, and the item is shoved in that space. With all the tubs stacked up in front, no one would ever see it unless they cleared the space. I dislodge it and find that it's a white, gauzy bag with a heavy object in it. I gently open the bag and almost drop it when I see what's in it. I gasp. It's a gun. No wonder it's so heavy. I locate the box of latex gloves I saw earlier. Removing the weapon with my gloved hands, I check to see if the gun is loaded. Sure enough, there is almost a full magazine inside. The M9 Beretta is the most common pistol used in the military. The bag contains a suppressor as well. The only reason I know this is because Jack taught me how to use the Beretta. Jack taught me a lot of things. I place the gun back in the bag and wedge it back in the corner.

*Why would Gemma have a gun?* And then it dawns on me. *Was this the gun used to kill the person in my basement? Did Gemma kill Scarlett? Was it an accident?* I can't put the pieces of the puzzle together. *Is Gemma a killer? But if she knew it was here, why would she ask me to reorganize the shed?* Panic bubbles up in my throat, and beads of sweat form on my brow. I hold on to the edge of the tub and slow my breaths. The baby kicks me hard, and I grab my belly. I remember Emilio's words about staying calm. I close my eyes and imagine he's there with me. The baby settles, and I place the contents of each tub back. The shed door creaks open, and I jump.

"Lemonade?" Gemma asks. She's carrying a tray with a pitcher, two glasses, and a plate of cookies. "I thought we could take a break and sit outside. Even in late August, the weather is warm here in Southern California. Are you okay? I'm not working you too hard, am I?"

I shake my head, wipe my brow, and urge myself to act normal until I figure out what to do.

"I don't want you over-exhausting yourself. None of these projects is so dire that they are more important than you and that baby of yours," Gemma says, walking over to the umbrella table. "Here. Sit."

"To tell you the truth, I love these projects," I tell her, a slight quiver in my voice. "The shed is quite a collection of different things."

Gemma smiles. "So, when I first met you, you had two names you were considering for the baby. Have you decided?"

I wrap my hands around my belly and say, "I have. Sebastian Emilio Caruso."

Gemma reaches over and takes my hands in hers. "I think that's a wonderful name. Emilio will love it."

# Chapter 35

Gemma

Fall is officially here. And you know what that means. No, no, not pumpkin spice lattes. It means another Sycamore potluck is in order. The leaves have turned magnificent shades of red, orange, and yellow. It's an ideal time to gather the neighbors of Sycamore together. Ali and I also agree that it would be the perfect cover for a surprise baby shower for Victoria. I tell Victoria I'm inviting the girls over to plan the Fall potluck. She's cleaned the place so meticulously; my countertops and floors sparkle like in the Mr. Clean commercials. The aromas of cinnamon and vanilla fill my home all day long.

Ali and Sydney are the first to arrive—Ali holds large bundles of baby blue balloons and a few foil balloons that say, "It's a Boy," and Sydney carries her polar bear. Sydney gravitates to Victoria and plops down on the couch next to her. Victoria's eyes grow big with excitement when she sees the balloons.

"Surprise!" Ali and Sydney say at the same time.

"Well, hello there, my little friend," Victoria says, hugging Sydney. "This is a pleasant surprise." And to Ali, who walks over and gives her a hug. "Thank you so much."

Sydney giggles and says, "Mama said we're having a surprise baby party today. Is he happy today?"

"I think so," Victoria says. "Would you like to ask him yourself?"

The excitement in Sydney's eyes says it all. She flings her bear down on the couch and gives Victoria both of her hands. Victoria places them on her belly and uses Sydney's hands to nudge the baby.

"He moved!" Sydney says as a huge smile spreads across her face. "I think he *is* happy today."

"I think you're right," Victoria tells her. "And guess what?"

"What?"

"I picked a name for him.'

"What is it?"

Victoria takes a deep breath as her eyes well up. She smiles and says, "Sebastian Emilio Caruso. What do you think?"

"I think that's a good name," Sydney says.

Victoria hugs Sydney and says, "Thank you, Sweetie. I'm glad you like it."

"There's a boy in my class named Sebastian," Sydney says. "We call him Seabass."

Victoria laughs. "And does he like his nickname?"

Sydney nods and says, "Uh-huh. He does. Everyone likes Seabass. He's smart and nice and funny."

I see Victoria light up as she hears this. "Well then, maybe that can be the baby's nickname, too."

Sydney smiles and says, "I like that." And to Victoria's belly, "Do you like it too?"

The doorbell rings. Darby and Penelope's arms are full of appetizers, fruit, and a large salad. Ramona holds a bag of Pepperidge Farm cookies. We say our hellos, and Penelope helps Ali and me in the kitchen while Darby and Ramona sit with Victoria and Sydney.

"Auntie Darby! Guess what the baby's name is!" Sydney says. "Seabass!"

Darby's eyes open wide. "Seabass? Is that a name?"

"Sebastian. Sebastian Emilio," Victoria explains.

"Auntie Darby, we're calling him Seabass. It's short for Sebastian," Sydney says, then heads to the kitchen. "I'll get bowls for snacks. C'mon, Ramona."

"Careful, careful," Ali tells Sydney as she swings her arm out to shield her daughter from the stove. "There's hot food here. Why don't you and Ramona help Auntie Gemma arrange the cookies on a platter after you wash up?"

"'Kay, Mommy," Sydney says. "Can me and Ramona have cookies now, though?"

"Cookies are for later. I'll fix you both a proper snack first. Now, go wash your hands," Ali says sternly.

"Those two could be twins," Victoria says.

Ali laughs. "You're not the first one to say that. Those two go together like bread and butter."

The two little girls bounded back into the kitchen.

"Hands clean?" Ali asks, and they both nod and show their freshly washed hands.

"Ok, here, have some carrots with hummus for now," Ali says. She dips two carrot rounds and hands them to the girls.

Sydney wrinkles her nose but takes the carrot anyway and takes a bite.

"Mm, that's pretty decent," she says. Ramona agrees with a nod.

I laugh. "Decent, huh? That's a big word for a little girl."

"Mommy says it all the time. If it's kind of good, it's decent."

"At least she's using the word correctly, Ali."

Ali laughs, "Six years old going on thirty."

As we prepare the food for the shower (of course, I bought too much of everything again), we catch up on subjects including the baby's movements, the latest episode of the viral medical thriller on Netflix, Brooks' whiskey obsession, and Seamus' food addiction.

"I'm not even kidding. He's so Irish that we have a house rule to always have corned beef and potatoes available. Even when it's not St. Paddy's Day," Darby says.

"I loved corned beef, but it's very salty to have all the time," Gemma says.

"I agree," Darby agrees. "On top of that, he loves chips and sour cream onion dip. The problem is he devours the whole thing."

"Geez. How's his blood pressure?" Penelope asks.

"Too high. The doctor told him that if he keeps eating like this, he'll die of a heart attack before he turns fifty."

"Yikes. Better give Seamus some tough love. You don't want him keeling over," I tell her.

"The question is, how do I do that? The man is so pig-head-ed."

Sydney and Ramona fly into the room with stuffed animals. Ironically, Ramona is holding a stuffed pig.

"Oink! Oink! Oink!" Ramona says.

I laugh so hard, wine comes out of my nose. I reach for a napkin as Ali and Darby burst into giggles. Victoria smiles politely, but I can tell her mind is on more pressing matters. I reach over to squeeze her hand, and she gives me a polite smile.

"I say we make Fiona in charge of the main dish for the potluck," Ali says. "Since she's not here."

"May I remind you that Fiona is the mother hen of this block? I might be the one who does the prepping for all of our fun events, but when the shit hits the fan, it's Fiona that we would all turn to. I don't think now is the time to piss her off," I say.

The ladies agree with me, and Ali rolls her eyes. "Okay, okay," she says.

"So, Gemma, how are things with Keith?" Darby asks.

"They're good. We're still getting to know one another, but I like him a lot," I tell the group.

"How's he' in the..." Ali says, but Penelope cuts her off.

"Ali! Stop it! Leave poor Gemma alone. We don't go asking you about your and Brooks' bedroom habits," Penelope says.

Ali laughs and says, "What bedroom habits? My husband is never home. He's in love with money, not his wife. I don't remember the last time we had sex. I live vicariously through Gemma and her hot new boy toy."

I roll my eyes at her and say, "Well, for your information, we haven't done it yet. So, there's nothing to tell. He is a good kisser, though."

The girls whistle like a bunch of construction workers, and I laugh.

"What are we, in high school? We've decided to take things slow," I tell them as I set up the baby shower games. "He had a few bad relationships and some traumatic experiences in his life. I'm fine with it. I've been single for this long. What's a few more months?" I tell them.

The conversation moves away from Keith and me to Penelope and Freddy.

"So, are you guys having any more kiddos?" Ali asks as she takes another sip of wine.

"Nope, I told Freddy I'm done. I'm happy with my two boys."

I glance over at Victoria, who is once again in a far-off place. I can't imagine how stressed she must feel without Emilio here and Sebastian on the way.

"Who's ready for games?" I ask, and Ramona and Sydney jump up and down in excitement.

This is the first time I've ever thrown a baby shower, and as I step back and take in the spread of food, drinks, and games on the table, I look around at my friends and take in this moment. Victoria smiles, but I can tell her mind is preoccupied. Her paranoia must be rubbing off on me because I look around to ensure that the windows and doors are locked. All we need is an angry husband showing up at the shower.

"Okay, first up, guess the baby food. Blindfolds on!"

# Chapter 36

Victoria

*What is that scratching noise? Where is it coming from?* I'm a tad discombobulated as I maneuver my way out of bed and open my bedroom door. Chester is at the front door. *Where's Gemma?*

"Hey, boy. Do you need to go out?" I ask. I open the front door, and he bolts outside to do his business on the lawn. *Poor guy, he must have had to go badly.* Chester comes back in, and I step outside with a poop bag to pick up his deposit. As I drop the bag into the outside trash bin, movement in the house next door, the one Emilio and I once shared, catches my eye. A shadow. Startled, I stumble back and slam the front door shut. I lock it behind me. Chester tilts his head at me, clearly thinking I've lost it. I busy myself and fill his water and food bowls, then creep toward the kitchen window. Maybe I'll catch another glimpse without being seen. I crouch low at the sink and slowly lift my head enough to peer outside. The shadow darts past again. It flashes from the kitchen into the other rooms. I hold my breath and listen. The house was nearly stripped bare after the fire, yet whoever is inside now is making an awful lot of noise.

I hear a man's grunt. Who could be inside the house? I continue watching out the window. The only car parked in the driveway is Emilio's Chevy.

"What are you doing?" a groggy voice says behind me. I turn to see Gemma in her bathrobe, hair disheveled, complexion ruddy.

"Are you okay?" I ask.

"I think I had too much fun last night," Gemma says. "I can't drink like I used to. A few glasses of wine and poof, hungover the next day."

"Coffee?"

"Yes, please. You're a dear."

I pour her a cup and make it how she likes it, with a splash of half and half. Gemma sits at the kitchen table. She observes Chester next to his bowl.

"Oh, shoot. What time is it?" Gemma glances at the clock. It's 8:00 a.m. She usually takes Chester out at 6:00 a.m.

"I woke up so late. Did he have an accident?" She says as she scans the house for puddles or poop.

"Almost. I heard him scratching, and he made it in the nick of time."

"Oh, boy, I'm so sorry, buddy," she leans down to scratch him on the head. He whimpers in acknowledgement. Gemma turns back to me. "So, what were you looking at a minute ago?"

My face turns red with embarrassment. I explain to her about the poop, the trash, and the man.

"I'm sure it's a contractor. Who else would be walking around in a burned-down house? Fiona said she would most likely demolish the building and then rebuild the house. It depends on the integrity of the foundation. Because the fire originated in the basement, they can't tell if the foundation is viable yet."

"I feel awful about it. We were there all of one month, and this happens."

"It's not your fault. You can't prove that it had to do with your soon-to-be ex. It's not like he showed up on your doorstep announcing his arrival. And you haven't seen anything since, right? You said you thought you saw his car before."

"You're right. I haven't. Everything has been quiet and normal. It almost makes me nervous how quiet it is."

"That's how things are supposed to be. No violence. No chaos. Just good people, good food, and good friends."

Gemma's right. I guess I've never known, only ever known chaos. It'll take a while to get used to living in peace. The gun is still at the forefront of my mind. For the past day, I've pep-talked myself out of believing that Gemma is complicit in a crime. Even though the gun was in her shed, it doesn't mean she put it there. Trying to act normal in front of Ali and Sydney last night was a challenge. I have no idea how to ask Gemma about it, but I need to. I'm tired of the secrets and pain that others have caused. I clear my throat.

Gemma turns to me and says, "What is it? Are you feeling okay?"

I take a deep breath and nod. *Here goes.*

"Can I ask you something, Gemma?"

"Of course, what is it?"

"Promise you won't get mad?"

I'm stalling now. I can't do it. She's my only friend, after all. *What if she kicks me out? What if she hates me for accusing her of something so heinous? And what if she did it?*

I take a seat on the couch."Okay, now you're scaring me. What did you do?"

"It's not that. I didn't do anything," I pause, then cover my face with my hands. Gemma takes my hands and holds them in hers. She sits next to me on the couch.

"Whatever it is, you can tell me. I'm your friend," she says.

I take a huge gulp of air, then spit out the words, "Did you? Did you kill Scarlett?"

# Chapter 37

Gemma

For a second, I think it's a joke. Did I kill Scarlett? *What? Is she serious?* From the expression on her face, she's clearly not kidding. I say to her, "What are you talking about?"

"Umm, did you kill her?" Victoria's face is red, as if she's about to pass out from not breathing. She can barely get the words out. "Or do you know who did?"

"Did I kill Scarlett?" I repeat. "No, why would you think that?"

"Because of the gun," she says, her voice a hoarse whisper.

"What gun?"

"The one in your shed."

"What gun in my shed? Okay, wait. You're asking me if I killed Scarlett because there is a gun in my shed?"

Victoria nods. Clearly, we are both confused. I grab her hand and say, "Show me."

As Victoria leads me to the shed, she repeats in a soft voice, "I'm sorry. I'm sorry."

This poor girl has already been through so much. I can't imagine what she's feeling right now. At the entrance of the shed, I turn her around and grasp both of her shoulders.

"I didn't kill Scarlett, okay?"

She nods, her eyes rimmed with red, and throws her arms around me in an embrace.

"Hey, hey, it'll be okay. We'll figure this out," I tell her. And I hope my cowardice doesn't show through because I'm about as scared as she looks. Although my dad was a cop, I've never been comfortable around guns. Victoria turns to open the shed door. I follow her in. She removed a tub from a stack in the corner of the shed.

"Here, let me do that," I tell her before she lifts another tub. She steps aside.

"It's in the corner. I found it when I was in here the other day," Victoria says, her voice shaky. "I thought..."

I see a white drawstring bag and reach to pick it up, but Victoria stops me.

"No! Don't. Here, put these on."

She opens a nearby tub and pulls out a pair of disposable latex gloves from a box, the ones I use for dyeing my hair. She hands them to me.

I pick the bag up. It's heavy. I look inside. Yep. It's a gun. That's for sure.

"The magazine is almost full," she says. "Only one bullet is missing."

"You...you mean."

"I think this was the gun used to kill Scarlett, or whoever the body was, in the basement."

"We should hand it over to the police," I tell her.

Victoria nods and says, "So, you had no idea about the gun?"

"No, of course not. But it scares me that someone put it in my shed. Who would do that?"

Victoria takes a deep breath and puts the bag on the ground.

"Oh, thank God," she says, giving me a hug. "Thank God it wasn't you. You're my only friend."

I hug her back. A lot has happened since Victoria and Emilio's arrival in Laurelville.

***

I call the police non-emergency number and tell them about the gun. They send an officer immediately to collect it. I take down the officer's badge number and last name, which is Adams. I can't help but wonder if the officer is related to Fiona.

# Chapter 38

Keith

"So now what?" I ask Fiona as she circles my kitchen table and places the paper bag down. Eventually, someone will become suspicious of her stopping by my place at all hours of the day and night. I told her to call me instead, but she's paranoid about someone being able to listen in. When Fiona came by after the fire, there were shadows in the house across the street. Someone saw us.

"Let me think," she tells me. But there isn't anger or frustration in her voice.

"Maybe we should move Victoria," I tell Fiona. "Until we find him."

"No, no, she's safer on Sycamore Way than anywhere else. She needs to be where we can keep an eye on her. It ended up working out for Margot and Sasha. Victoria will be fine as well.

She's vulnerable because she's pregnant. We must remember that. We need to be smart. No more deviating from the plan.

"I can't believe you burned your own house down," I tell her. "Why didn't you call me to dispose of the body?"

"It was too risky if we got caught," Fiona says.

"They still haven't identified either set of bones."

"And hopefully it stays that way."

"And how did you get this?" I ask, holding up the bag with the gun in it.

"Gator called me. Gemma called in a gun she discovered on her property. He went to collect it. It was pure luck that he was the one who took the call. I have a feeling this might be the gun that killed the woman in the basement."

"So, who was she?"

"That's a good question. We'll find out. Eventually."

Fiona pulls out her phone. She opens the camera app to show me photos and a video she took of the body before she scorched the place.

"I can't believe you took these," I tell her. "You know how bad it would be if these got into the wrong hands? Erase those."

Fiona ignores my remarks and says, "Does she look familiar to you?"

"What? No. How would I know who that is?"

"Can't you do something on your phone like Google her to find out?"

Now it's my turn to ignore her question.

"How did you know there was a dead body in your base-ment?"

"What?"

"You knew there was a body down there. That's why you burned the house down, right? To get rid of the evidence?"

"Right."

"So, what, you were hanging out in the basement of the house and stumbled upon a freshly killed body?"

Fiona looks at me as if I've grown a second head.

"Did you kill her, Fiona? You may as well tell me if you did or not."

"No, of course I didn't kill her. I don't even know who she is. For goodness 'sake, Keith. Do you think I go around murdering strangers and putting their bodies in the basements of my own houses?"

I laugh. "Maybe I should check the basement of this house."

"Don't be a smartass. Sometimes you must do things for the sake of the greater good. Even if it means bending the law. You of all people know that, Keith. Now, I'm sending you these photos. You do whatever it is you kids do and find out who this woman is and what she was doing snooping around my house. And while you're at it, find Tony."

"Yes, mother."

***

Growing up with Fiona Adams as a stepmother was no easy feat. Although she's calm and put together on the outside, she also demands a lot of those around her. After my mother died when I was a kid, my father fell into a deep bout of depression. He became a different person. It was a blessing that he was gone a lot for the National Guard. Although he was militant, I knew he loved my brother and me. He was blindsided by our mother's death and wasn't equipped to handle two active boys. Her death was sudden, and although he wouldn't give us the details, he was the one who had found her in the house. Five years after my mother's death, my dad met Fiona on a dating site. He liked her because she was an independent woman capable of earning her own money and taking care of herself. If you ask me, their relationship was more like a business agreement. Don't get me wrong, Fiona is an attractive lady. Her strong personality and independence made her charismatic, traits I think my dad admired—at least at first. And she was a good stepmother. I have no idea how she raised us boys, without going insane. We were wild. I guess that's why we both ended up in the military.

# Chapter 39

VICTORIA

Jack wasn't always a jerk. Sexy, muscular, manly, and protective. He was all that a girl would want. At least that's what I thought. Until I got pregnant, he treated me like a trophy wife. Sure, we didn't have tons of money, but with my job as a nurse and his as a mechanic, we did well for ourselves. As soon as my belly showed, it was as if a switch had been flipped. He no longer gave me loving glances. He was full of anger. Jack became a different person.

One day, I thought I would surprise him at the shop with a picnic lunch. I put on my new yellow dress, made and packed his favorite sandwiches, turkey and Swiss on rye, and headed down to the shop. It was my day off on Wednesdays, and I enjoyed having a day to myself. Sometimes Jack would leave work early to spend time with me. But after I got pregnant, that stopped.

"What are you doing here?" he asked. He glared at my belly in disgust.

I was about four and a half months pregnant, and his behavior had gotten worse. I couldn't figure out why he was so angry. Although the pregnancy was a surprise, we had discussed having children before we were married, and he was all for it. So, why was Jack acting like this?

"I brought us lunch. I thought we could sit over at the picnic table over there and share it. I made your favorite sandwiches and brought your favorite soda, A&W Root beer."

"I already took my lunch," he said, as he brushed past me and knocked into my shoulder.

"It's not even 11:30 a.m.," I told him.

"Yeah, so? I took it early. Maybe Tony over there wants to have lunch with you. Since you like him so much," he said.

"Are you serious? Are you jealous of Tony? He's *your* friend, Jack."

Jack looked up at me. "Just get out of here. I'm busy."

I ran to the car and sped home. I didn't know what had happened to my loving husband. Because this man was not him.

Things got progressively worse. First, it was little shoves and rough sex, then the emotional abuse set in. He called me all the names in the book. I never knew what would trigger him. One time, I came home late from work after a twenty-four-hour shift. A van full of musicians had fallen over a cliff in Half Moon Bay, and they were brought in an hour before my shift ended. The hospital needed more hands, so I stayed late. When I arrived back home, exhausted, I figured Jack would be asleep. When I pulled into our driveway, five months pregnant, he was waiting for me. He swung my car door open, and before I could say anything, Jack yanked me out from the driver's seat. My limbs were tangled in my seatbelt at that point, and I landed on the driveway with one foot still caught in it. He kicked me in the back repeatedly. I had no choice but to protect my belly and yell for him to stop. The kicks landed in my lower back. I thought my kidneys would explode as he belted out words like "bitch" and "slut." Eventually, he stopped and stormed back upstairs into the apartment. I lay there and cried, hoping my baby was okay.

After that, Jack resorted to a myriad of antics. He would choke me on the couch until I almost lost consciousness, smack me in the back of the head when I turned away from him, and shove me whenever he felt like it. It wasn't until Tony said something to me that I realized other people noticed the abuse, too.

Tony, Scarlett, and a few other friends from Jack's shop were over for a barbecue. Tony pulled me aside after Jack had gone indoors to retrieve something from the apartment.

"Cara, does he hurt you?" he asked me.

I was taken aback at first, but it was what I saw in Tony's eyes that made me feel like I could trust him. Kindness.

"I'm fine," I whispered. I didn't want Tony to worry about me. "I can handle it."

"Cara, you have a black eye. And last week you had bruises on your arms," Tony said.

"Don't tell anyone, okay? Jack would kill me if anyone found out. I thought I did well with covering the bruises up," I told him. Jack taught me how to use theatrical makeup to cover the bruises. If someone noticed them, I would gaslight them. Jack was skilled at pretending to be someone he wasn't. He taught me how to be as fake as he was. I thought white lies were no big deal. Now I'm appalled at my behavior.

"I saw the bruises when you changed from your sweater to your jacket last weekend. You *have* been doing an unbelievable job of hiding them. But that's not the point. How long has this been happening?" Tony asked me.

"Around two months. It began when my belly began to show," I said.

"It won't get better, Cara. I can help you."

"Help me? How?"

"Do you trust me?"

I nodded. Tony and I agreed to meet the following Wednesday at a small café in a town two cities over. This is where Tony told me about the plan to become Victoria and Emilio.

# Chapter 40

Gemma

"Hey," Ali says. "You're in time for snacks with Sydney. Today, we have fruit salad and homemade buttermilk biscuits courtesy of Pillsbury.

I giggle. "You are such a mom. I should write a children's book about you and all your mommish things."

"It would be a bestseller, that's for sure," Ali says as she pops a grape into her mouth. "So, what did you want to talk about? You sounded so serious and cryptic on the phone. Is it about Victoria?"

Before I can answer, Sydney strolls into the room with her polar bear.

"Hi, Auntie Gemma. I'm back from school," Sydney says. "Brodie's mom drove us today."

Sydney's energy lights up the room, and she hugs Ali and me, then takes her snack tray into the living room. She flips the TV on to watch some cartoons.

"Mind if we sit outside?" I ask Ali.

Ali gives me a look. She knows I have something serious to ask her—something that might not be safe for little ears.

"So, what's up?" Ali says as she serves us the refreshments.

"You like Victoria, right?"

"Uh, sure. She seems nice. Like one of us. Uh oh, Gem. Did something happen?"

I fill Ali in on Victoria's ex and how she's running from him. I also tell her about the gun we found.

"Do you think she's hiding something?" Ali asks me.

"I know she is. I think she's more scared than she lets on. She thinks the woman who was killed in her basement is her best friend. Well, ex-best friend. They had a falling out."

Ali taps her fingernails on the picnic table for a few seconds. "You know what I think?"

"Hmm? Please tell."

"I think you need to watch your back. Her ex sounds like a bad guy, someone you don't want to mess with."

"Didn't you tell me that you were in a bad relationship before you met Brooks?" Gemma asks.

"Yes. Am I sure glad I got out of that. My ex put me through the wringer. I'm so glad I met Brooks. He would never lay a finger on me." Ali says. I notice as she rubs the goosebumps on her arms, and I feel bad that I've conjured up terrible memories for her.

"I'm sorry I brought it up," I say.

"No, it's fine. My therapist taught me how to compartmentalize, which has helped with the PTSD. When someone tries to take your life, well, that's something you don't forget."

I reach over and grab her hand and squeeze it. "We can stop talking about it."

"No, no. Ask away. It actually helps me to talk about it. The more I talk about it, the further away I can push it into the past. Almost like it happened to someone else. Does that make sense?"

I nod. "How did you get away from him? Did you run away and change your name?"

Ali takes a sip of her water and puts the glass down. "When I moved, it wasn't because of my ex. It was because I wanted to reinvent myself. Start anew."

"You weren't afraid your ex would track you down?"

"I'm a stronger person because of what I went through. I thought he would kill me those last couple of months. Sometimes I remind myself every day that I don't have to look over my shoulder anymore. I never have to worry about him again."

"Why not?" Gemma asks.

"Because I killed him."

***

The revelation that my best friend, Ali, could kill a man leaves me at a loss for words. Of course, who am I to judge? I've never been in an abusive relationship. Hearing both Victoria's and Ali's stories makes me admire their courage and strength. Victoria's soon-to-be ex-husband, Jack, sounds a lot like Ali's ex-boyfriend, Johnny. From what Ali told me, Johnny tortured her with things like suffocation with a plastic bag over her head, putting her in a headlock, and shoving his knee into her spine. Like Victoria's ex, he also liked to leave bruises. Ali said he taught her how to cover them up and lie to people about it. As a last resort, she stabbed him in their home, making sure she cut him deep and dragging the knife down from his chest to his belly. Her memory of running that night and the person who helped her was fuzzy and hidden somewhere deep in the back of her mind.

# Chapter 41



Gemma

I prepare dinner to bring to Keith's house. Ali's words swirl around in my mind. Victoria is napping in her room. I lock the door behind Chester and me, and we head to Keith's house.

Keith answers the door and gives me a peck on the cheek. I follow him into the kitchen, where I'm surprised to see Fiona. She's nursing a glass of wine.

"Oh! Fiona, how are you?" I ask.

"Gemma, dear. Wonderful to see your smiling face. I was giving Keith here a few more house projects to work on."

"If you'd like to stay for dinner, I made plenty of food. Zucchini taco boats with Mexican street corn salad."

"That sounds delicious. Maybe next time, though. I have some office paperwork I need to catch up on," Fiona says, moving over to the sink and rinsing her wine glass.

Keith has a relieved expression on his face.

As Fiona steps out the front door, Keith says, "I think you forgot something, Fiona."

He shoves a crumpled paper bag toward her, and Fiona grabs it.

"Oops. Thank you. Can't forget that," she says. "See you both later."

As she turns back around with the bag, I could swear I see a white drawstring peeking out from the top of the bag. I guess I called that one. It can't be a coincidence that the officer who came to pick up the white bag with the gun has the same last name as Fiona, and now Fiona is over at Keith's house with that same white bag. The question is, why would she want the gun? *Is it hers? Did she kill the person in Victoria's basement? And how is Keith mixed up in all of this?* My intuition tells me to run, but I don't know how.

All through dinner, I can't stop thinking about the gun. I want to ask Keith, but I can't come up with the right questions without sounding like I'm a nosy neighbor. I zone out at least three times.

"Are you okay?" Keith asks.

"Sorry, I'm worried about Victoria. She's gone through so much. I told her not to give up hope that Emilio is still alive. I think they really loved each other."

Keith has no expression on his face. No sign of warmth or sympathy. No sign of anything, really. Does he know they weren't married?

"Uh, yeah, that's too bad. They still haven't figured out the identity of the dead body at the house?"

"No, the body was so burned they're having a hard time extracting the DNA. The report said it was a female, though, so it couldn't have been Emilio."

"Hmm," Keith says, and I can't get a read on him. I decided to probe him a bit with some questions.

"Don't you think it's odd how Emilio disappeared?" I ask.

"Well, yeah. It is."

"What could have happened? A person can't disappear out of thin air."

"No. You're right. Maybe Emilio decided this wasn't what he wanted anymore."

"And leave Victoria and the baby?"

Keith shrugs. "What did Victoria say about it?"

"Victoria's as confused as I am. Emilio left the car keys. That means it was premeditated, right?"

"Maybe he's having an internal crisis. You said they're new to the street, right? Sometimes people have secrets, Gemma. Even the people we like."

"You're right. I worry about Victoria and the baby being all alone. Baked goods and Shepherd's Pie can only fix so much."

"You're so much more than baked goods and Shepherd's Pie, Gemma. Victoria is lucky to have you as a friend."

I reach for my glass of wine and take a sip. My phone rings. It's Victoria.

"Hey," I answer. "Are you okay?"

"Gemma? I'm so sorry to bother you and interrupt your time with Keith. I think my water broke."

I jump up and scream in excitement. I think everyone on the block heard me because I see Ali and Sydney run out as I open Keith's front door.

"Victoria's water broke!"

Ali squeals, then shoos me toward my house and says, "I'll pack a care package and meet you at the hospital. Go!"

The few steps down the street seem like an eternity. I reach the threshold of my front entryway, where Victoria and I almost collide with one another. We both giggle, and I hug her.

"Are we doing this or what?" I tell her. "Let's go have a baby!"

# Chapter 42

KEITH

Dammit. I'm almost positive Gemma saw the bag I gave my mom on her way out. That was a mistake. I'm glad she didn't ask about it, although I could tell it was on her mind all afternoon. Fiona is right. The plan is falling apart, and I'll be damned if the woman I care about gets hurt. I wonder how much Victoria has told her about Emilio. Although Gemma has Chester, I feel the need to protect her. Each house I have done repairs on has cameras. They're not placed perfectly, but they'll get the job done. I can see who arrives and leaves from all angles on Sycamore. The only house that doesn't have cameras is Gemma's. I probably should have just asked her. I'm one hundred percent sure she would have said yes, but I didn't want to raise her suspicions of the danger that could be lurking on Sycamore Way.

Now that my neighbors are preoccupied—Gemma and Victoria are at the hospital, Ali and Darby are at Ali's house putting together God knows what to bring to the hospital, and everyone else is at work—I'll take the opportunity to get it done.

Chester and I enter Gemma's house with the key she gave me to the back door. I follow him to the kitchen, where I give him a treat. Chester is a good boy and an even better guard dog. I'm thankful that Gemma and Chester have allowed me into their world. When we're together, it feels right. Chester and I practice his commands in the backyard often, and he's learned to trust me.

I installed the micro cameras to face each entryway—the front, back, and garage doors, and each window. You can never be too careful. I open the app to test the camera angles. The guy I bought them from swore they were top-of-the-line, and he was right.

# Chapter 43

VICTORIA

Why don't mothers warn new mothers about how painful it is to give birth? The pushing isn't even the hard part. I don't know why they call it labor because you can't do anything but lie there in the worst pain imaginable. The little line on the graph creeps up, and I prepare myself for the next contraction. How big would this one be, and why am I only three centimeters dilated after two hours? This little guy sure is taking his sweet time. I massage my belly and practice a breathing technique I learned on YouTube. Ali and Darby stop by with some finger foods, which Gemma has been munching on since I'm not allowed to eat. I take a few spoonfuls of ice chips, which help to wet my palate. I'm glad Gemma is with me. She calls Keith to give him an update. I feel bad about interrupting their dinner.

As I take deep inhales and let them out slowly, the contraction reaches its peak. Each one feels like a pair of giant hands wringing my insides out. I lie on my side with a pillow under my belly, which helps relieve a bit of the pressure. I squeeze the hospital bed railing with each contraction.

"Hi, Honey," a nurse says in a soothing tone. "Time to check again, okay?"

I nod as she reaches a gloved hand up inside me. You would think someone would have come up with a device to measure dilation from the outside by now.

"Five centimeters," she says, as if she's the proud parent of a student who achieved an A on her math test.

Well, at least five is better than three.

# Chapter 44



As I watch Victoria give birth, it makes me question if I ever want to have children. She's in pain for hours before they gave her the epidural. Finally, when she's dilated ten centimeters, two nurses and a doctor stroll in and tell her it's time to push. Although we were there for what seemed like an eternity, when it came time for her to push, I don't think I was ready for what was about to happen. Not at all. Honestly, I don't think Victoria was prepared for it either. This is one of those things you can't take back. The baby is coming no matter what.

At eight pounds four ounces, Sebastian is a hefty little guy. His cries are music to our ears, and a tear slips down Victoria's cheek as her head hits the pillow, exhausted. The nurses bathe the baby in a small tub and wrap him in a blanket. Almost immediately, he takes to Victoria's breast and feeds as if he were starving. Later, as I rock Sebastian in my arms, Victoria looks up with tired eyes and smiles. She says in a hoarse voice, "Thank you, Gemma. Love you." Before I can answer back, her eyes shut, and she falls into a peaceful slumber. Sebastian falls sound asleep like his mama, his little lips twitching. I take time to enjoy this moment.

***

I have to say, Victoria is one tough cookie. Probably tougher than I give her credit for. She is ready to leave the hospital within a few hours of delivering Sebastian. The nurses insist she stay in the hospital for at least twenty-four hours before she can be discharged. She says her lady parts still feel a little numb. We both laugh after I say, "Well, you did squeeze a tiny person out of there! Have you seen the size of his head?"

I spent the night in Victoria's hospital room, even though she told me I could go home. With everything that has happened with her ex-husband, and without Emilio there and with her being in such a vulnerable state, I wouldn't feel right leaving her by herself.

The next evening, I call Keith right before we are ready to leave the hospital. Sycamore is a five-minute drive away, so I ask him to meet us at my place. As we pull onto Sycamore Way, Keith is in my driveway, Chester by his side. Keith opens Victoria's car door and helps her out.

"Slow," he says, as he guides her by the arm and elbow.

"Thanks," she says. "I think that's the only speed I can move right now."

"Take your time," Keith says. I like this man more and more. There's something about a manly man who shows his gentle side. My mind drifts off to what he would be like as a father. I shake the thoughts out of my head. *What are you thinking, Gemma? You hardly know the man.*

I remove the car seat carrier and follow Keith and Victoria inside. Keith helps Victoria onto the couch. I place a snoozing Sebastian on the sofa next to her. He's so peaceful, wrapped in a blanket and tucked into the carrier. His little chest expands with each baby breath. Keith bends over to inspect and whispers, "Cute little guy. Congratulations."

Victoria nods and mouths, "Thanks." She rocks the carrier gently, humming a soft tune. Keith and I leave the room to give her some space. Keith sits at my kitchen table and gives me an update on his handyman jobs. I pour us each a glass of lemonade and give Chester a treat.

"Ginny asked you to do work? As in Mrs. Nelson? Did you know she's one hundred and two years old?"

"Wow, that's quite a lifetime. It was her caregiver, Molly, who contacted me for a few small fix-it projects."

"Back when I first moved here, Ginny would sit out on her front porch and knit. Molly's a sweetheart. She loves Ginny like a mother."

Keith laughs. "You're too much, Gemma. Your knowledge of everyone and everything in this neighborhood sure is impressive."

I blush. "Not everyone. I don't know that much about you."

"We can change that," he says, leaning over to kiss me.

# Chapter 45

Victoria

Sebastian is a fantastic sleeper from the start. This is both pleasant and unexpected. He wakes up every two hours to feed. I change his diaper, and he falls right back asleep. With his bassinet right next to my bed, it makes nighttime feedings easier.

One night, I hear a sound from out in the living room or kitchen. I glance at the bedside clock. 3:00 a.m. Maybe Gemma couldn't sleep. *Should I go out there to see? Or should I stay in the bedroom in case it's an intruder?* I lock my door each night as a safety precaution, in case Jack shows up. As I contemplate what to do, I listen for more sounds. A soft thud makes my heart flutter. *Gemma might be in trouble.* I roll over to the opposite side of the queen bed and open the nightstand drawer. I'm hoping to find something substantial enough to defend myself if needed. What I find is unexpected...a cell phone.

I remove it from the drawer and power it up. It's not until I see the Apple ID that I realize this is Emilio's phone. *Why would his phone be in Gemma's house?* My stomach sinks. I don't believe Gemma is a bad person, but after the gun and now this, you can't help but blame me, right?

I search through the phone, moving from one application to the next. First, I check the phone call list. Empty. Next, the iMessages and text messages. Also, empty. I check the Notes app. That's where I see it.

**V-**

**I'm so sorry. I never meant to hurt Scarlett. I panicked when I thought the noise I heard in the basement was an intruder. I thought it was Jack. I am watching you and Sebastian from afar. If Jack shows up, I will be there. I love you so much. I always have. I will explain when I see you again.**

**-E.**

My heart drops to the pit of my stomach as I read Emilio's message repeatedly. *How did he get this phone into Gemma's house? And how can he be watching from afar? Is he here on Sycamore? Who told him the baby's name? Think, Victoria, think.*

***

It's 6:00 a.m., and Sebastian stirs in his bassinet. He smiles and coos at me, and I kiss his little nose. He's truly the most precious thing I have ever laid eyes on. He feeds, burps, and then poops. I lay him down on the bed and undo his swaddle to change his diaper.

"Eww, who did this?" I tease him and tickle his belly as I change him. "Who did a stinky poopy?"

Sebastian gurgles. Although it's officially fall, the air still carries its summer warmth, so I wrap him in a light blanket. I stop before I open the door to the bedroom. Still thinking about the strange noises last night, I slowly open the door and peek out.

"Good morning, sleepy heads," Gemma says from the kitchen when she hears my door open. I take a sigh of relief as she makes me a cup of peppermint tea and adds a splash of almond milk.

"Good morning, Auntie Gemma," I say in a baby voice, and wave Sebastian's little arm at her. I look around the house, and nothing appears out of the ordinary. No sign of a break-in or scuffle.

"Did he even wake up last night?" she asks.

"Yep, twice—to eat and have his diaper changed. Then, he fell right back asleep."

"Wow, what a good boy," Gemma says as she kisses Sebastian on the head. Chester barks to remind us he's there, too. "And you're a good boy too, Chester."

"Hey, Gem?" I ask.

"Yeah, what's up? Are you feeling okay?"

"Mm, hmm. I'm fine. But by any chance did you get up at 3:00ish?"

"Oh, sorry. Yep, that was me. Did I wake you? I woke up absolutely parched in the middle of the night. I dropped the bottle of water as I grabbed for it. Clumsy me."

A wave of relief washes over me. "Whew. I'm glad it was you. You *were* quiet. I think I sleep lighter now, ever since Sebastian's birth. And with Emilio's disappearance. I'm glad it was you and not an intruder."

"Ahh, yes, that was me. Of course, I ended up having to pee multiple times afterward, so I'm surprised you didn't hear me then, too."

"No, I passed out after..." I trail off, remembering last night.

"After?"

"Gem, I need to show you something."

# Chapter 46

Gemma

I follow Victoria into the bedroom, and she hands me a phone. I'm confused at first, but then I tap the screen to unlock it. A message in the Notes app appears, and I read it three times before I understand.

"Whose phone is this?" I ask her.

"It's Emilio's. I found it in the bedside drawer."

"In my house?"

Victoria nods.

"How did it get there?" I ask, confused.

"I was going to ask you the same thing. It must be someone who has a key to your place if it wasn't you, right?" Victoria asks.

"It wasn't me. The only person who has a spare key to the back door is Keith. I gave it to him in case of an emergency. I have a key to his house, too. How would he have gotten Emilio's phone?"

"Hey, Gemma?"

"Yeah?"

"You've been here ten years on Sycamore, right?"

I nod.

"Do you ever feel like you're being watched?"

Goosebumps rise on my arms. I guess I'm not the only one who feels the energy of this neighborhood. Darby told me a while back that the energy in this neighborhood has a strong pull, and sometimes she feels the need to distance herself from everyone. Because she's a healer and an empath, she can absorb the positive and negative energy around her easily. She uses herbs and oils to do daily cleanses and rituals. Maybe Darby might be onto something.

"You do, don't you?" Victoria says, and I snap out of my trance.

I nod. "Keith knows something. I'm not sure what. Fiona too. I didn't tell you because we didn't get a chance to talk before you went into labor, but when I went over to Keith's house the other day, Fiona was there. And she had the gun with her."

"The gun? The one you turned into the police?"

I nod.

There is a long silence as Victoria and I stare at one another, trying to put the pieces of the puzzle together. I read the phone message for the fourth time.

"Okay, so according to this message, Emilio is watching you. *And* he was the one who killed Scarlett in your basement. Why did he burn the house down? And where is he now?"

"Your guess is as good as mine, but if Keith is the only one who has a key to your house, and he knows about the gun, I say we start there."

# Chapter 47

KEITH

"What the fuck, man? What were you thinking? Fiona said she saw someone run from the house and assumed it was Jack. It was you? You're lucky we could intercept the gun before anyone else found out. You left several partial prints on it. Gator answered the call. What the hell happened?"

Tony and I sit in the parking lot of the Hobby Lobby in Locke City. His eyes look down as he tells me what happened the day he left one woman asleep on the couch as he killed another woman in the basement.

"I messed up. Cara was asleep, and I heard a noise. I tracked it to the basement. I thought it was Jack hiding out. Man, you might have grown up with him, but I worked with him. And I saw how he treated Cara. That guy belongs in a mental institution."

"So, who was the woman? The police still don't know, and I couldn't find her from an online search."

"It was Scarlett, Cara's best friend."

"So, when you saw it was her and not Jack, why did you pull the trigger?"

Tony looks at me the same way Lars looked at me when he did something he shouldn't have.

"Spill it, Tony. You and I haven't known each other for long, but you must know by now that we're on the same team."

Tony covers his face with his hands. "I love Cara. I've been trying to convince her that we belong together. If Scarlett showed up, it would ruin everything."

It takes me a minute to figure out what he's talking about.

"I don't get it. What does Scarlett...oh shit. Did you hook up with Scarlett?"

Tony grabs my arm and says, "Don't tell her. You can't tell Cara. She would never forgive me. We were drunk one night, and Jack and Cara had gone to bed. It was only the one time."

"So, you thought we would be better off if you got rid of Scarlett?"

"I panicked. I thought she was here to ruin things between Cara and me. I've never killed anyone before. When I realized what I did, I wiped the prints off the gun the best I could and stashed it in a small hole in Gemma's shed. No one was supposed to find it."

"Why didn't you tell Fiona or me? Fiona found the body and assumed Jack killed her. We could have helped you. Instead, you ran. Fiona burned the house down because of you."

"If I stayed around, they would have tested me for GSR. I had to get out of there. I'm sorry, okay? I still don't understand why Fiona felt it necessary to burn the house down."

"There are secrets in that house. If Fiona hasn't told you about it, well, you may as well forget it and be thankful that you don't know."

Tony raises an eyebrow in question, and I give him a shake of my head to drop it. I'm not telling him Fiona's business. I only met the guy a few months ago, after all. Tony is Fiona's son with her first husband. I had never met him before moving to Laurelville. In fact, I had no idea he even existed before this. Fiona never mentioned him to Jack or me. According to her, he was sent to live with his aunt in Italy when he was a baby so she could focus on her career. It's ironic that Fiona raised my brother and me, but not her own kid. Tony isn't a bad guy. He is a bit naïve, though. I was surprised he could get Victoria out of Jack's grasp at all.

"You know what's weird?" he says.

"What's that?"

"You and Jack look so much alike. When Victoria and I first moved here, she thought you were him. She was ready to run."

"Gemma said Victoria thought I was Jack, too. I'm surprised she didn't ask if I know him. Maybe it's because my last name is different. When Fiona planned for my move to Sycamore, she let me keep my first name but changed my last name. I'm now Keith Schaffer."

"Speaking of Fiona, maybe we should call our dear mother," I say, as I take out my phone to dial. "She's the one who got both of us into this predicament. All these secrets and lies are scattered about. I'm sure Fiona has a plan to fix it. She was the only one who had ever gotten a handle on Jack."

***

I explain to Fiona where I am and that Tony is safe. I tell her about Scarlett. For once, Fiona has no words, although I can tell from her silence that she's pissed. I'm ready to come to Tony's defense. I mean, he's sort of like a little brother to me, even though we're not blood-related. And he's a lot easier to defend than Jack was. Jack was a bad seed from day one. Pure evil. Our father thought Jack would change his ways after a stint in the Army, but it seemed to make him worse. His violent outbursts came out of nowhere. I guess the apple doesn't fall far from the tree.

"Okay, bring him over to Gator's house. I'll tell Sheila you're on your way. We'll figure it out from there," she says.

Our cousin, Gator Adams, is Fiona's ex-husband's nephew. He's the Laurelville officer who came to pick up the gun, so we can trust him. Being in a small town gives law enforcement a lot of leeway in their processes, and not everything is done by the book. In fact, most of it isn't.

Gator's wife answers the door and greets us with a smile.

"Well, hello, you two. Keith, it's been a while. And you must be Tony. It's a pleasure to finally meet you," Sheila says, as she glances over our shoulders. "It's only you two, right?"

This question doesn't surprise me at all. Anyone who has met Jack knows he's trouble.

"Yes, ma'am. It's only us," Tony says. "It's a pleasure to meet you as well. We're sorry to intrude. Once Fiona gives us some instructions, we'll be out of your hair."

"Speak for yourself," I tell him. "I've got to get back and do my job, otherwise the boss will not be happy."

That makes Sheila laugh. "Good ole, Fiona. Are you sure I can't get you anything before you leave? Lemonade? A sand-wich?"

"Oh, no, I'm fine, Honey. Thank you," I tell her, and then turn to Tony. "And you. You stay out of sight until Fiona tells you otherwise, you hear?"

Tony nods, and I give him a pat on the back. "Thanks again, Sheila. Tell Gator I say hi."

"Will do, Keith."

I get back into my truck and stop at the 7-Eleven to grab a Gatorade and a bag of Doritos for the ride back. The road from Locke City to Laurelville is winding, which makes the drive seem longer than the forty minutes it truly takes. I'm about ten minutes away when my phone rings. The Caller ID says: Fiona.

"What's up? I'm on my way home."

"Keith?" she says, her voice quivering. "He's here."

The line drops.

# Chapter 48

Victoria

"Hey, do you want to come with me to Keith's? He said I could use his kitchen to try out some recipes for this weekend's potluck. His kitchen is larger and newer than mine, plus he has that industrial-sized fridge," Gemma calls to me from the kitchen.

I peek my head out of her guest bedroom, my head wrapped up in a towel.

"Sure! I'll throw some clothes on and be ready in a few," I tell her.

"No rush. I'm still packing all the stuff up."

We walk down to Keith's house with Chester and Sebastian in tow. It's nice to get some fresh air after being cooped up inside. Gemma pulls a wagon full of groceries and baking dishes. Sebastian snoozes in his front carrier pack, and I lean down to kiss the top of his head. His tiny pink lips quiver, and the corners of his mouth turn up. Is it a smile or maybe gas? I laugh to myself. But then I see it. A tiny dimple on his left cheek. The same as Jack. A sinking feeling dives to the pit of my belly, and reality hits me. This sweet, adorable little baby is still part Jack. But Jack isn't here to enjoy this moment. And he won't be here to enjoy any of these moments because he doesn't deserve Sebastian or me. Since running away, I've thought about what went wrong in our relationship. No matter how hard I try to figure it out, I still have no clue what made Jack spiral out of control.

My thoughts shift to Tony and how he saved Sebastian and me. I wish he were here to meet Sebastian. Tony kept us safe all these months. I hope he's okay. I recall the note on the phone. My eyes scan the neighborhood as I wonder if he's watching us now.

Gemma and I arrive on Keith's front porch, and Gemma knocks.

"Where's Keith's truck?" I ask. The driveway is empty.

"Silly me," Gemma says. "He told me he had to run out for an errand and to let myself in. Now, where is that key? I knew I should have put it on my keychain the day he gave it to me."

We stand on the porch. I hum as I rock Sebastian, while Gemma vigorously digs through her purse for the key. I look around the neighborhood and take in the quiet, peacefulness of the small town. When my eyes reach Fiona's house, I almost have a heart attack. There, in Fiona's driveway, is a flash of blue paint. I squint my eyes to make sure they're not playing tricks on me. It's Jack's car. My body freezes.

"Found it," she says as she holds up the key.

I whisper, "Gemma, we have to go. Now. Anywhere."

She follows my gaze and sees the blue car as well.

"Come on," she whispers, and we hustle to the back of Keith's house. She unlocks the French doors. Chester and I hurry into the house, and Gemma pulls the wagon in behind her. She shuts the back doors and locks them.

"What do we do?" I ask Gemma. I'm panicking, and every thought that has ever come across my mind as to what I would do if Jack showed up is now gone.

"I'm calling Keith," she says.

The phone rings and then goes to voicemail. Gemma sends a text: Call me ASAP. Victoria's ex is at Fiona's.

She tries again, but it goes straight to voicemail. Keith must be on the line with someone else.

"I wish I knew the number for that police officer who has the same last name as Fiona," Gemma says. "Maybe I should call the police department."

"Fiona!" I say. "Try calling Fiona. His car is in her driveway after all."

Gemma dials Fiona's cell number. It rings for what seems like an eternity before forwarding Gemma to voicemail. She tries Fiona's house phone, but the machine picks up.

Gemma peers out the window.

"Shoot. Neither Seamus nor Brooks is home," she says as her nails tap rhythmically on the marble countertop.

The screech of tires pierces the air, and Gemma and I peek through the curtain.

"He's leaving," Gemma says.

Jack's blue car peels out of Fiona's driveway and down Sycamore. I'm glad none of the kids are outside right now because Jack is a maniac. I know that rage.

Gemma and I stand in the middle of Keith's living room. My palms are sweaty, and my heart thumps as loud as a drum. Should we check on Fiona? Within a few minutes, another set of tires comes screeching onto the street.

"Is he back? What do we do? Call the police?" I ask her, following her to the front window again. "Why would Jack leave and then come back? I don't understand."

"It's Keith. He's in front of Fiona's," Gemma says. "He must have gotten my message."

# Chapter 49

Keith

"Fiona! Fiona!" I call out, worried about what I'll find. Dear God, I hope she's okay. I would never forgive myself if something happened to her. The front door is ajar, and I burst through it, ready for whatever comes my way. "Fiona!" I yell one more time.

"In here," I hear a weak voice say.

I sprint up the stairs toward Fiona's voice and find her in her bedroom, tied to a chair with duct tape. Makeup runs down her face as I undo the tape, and she reaches to wrap her arms around my neck. I hold Fiona tight as she sobs into my shoulder.

"Oh, Keith. Oh, baby, I'm so sorry," she says. "I was so careful to procure those IDs for Cara and Tony. That's why I made them stay two months on the road. I even took Victoria's burner phone to make sure she hadn't called Jack or anyone back home during their time on the run."

"It's not your fault," I tell her. "Victoria called Scarlett with the new phone. Of course, the area code led him right here. He knows Victoria is here. He'll come back. What did he say?"

"He asked me where she was, and I played stupid. He banged me around, but I fought back. I'm okay. A bit shaken," Fiona said, her body trembling, a reaction of her adrenaline levels as they drop. "He said he would go to the police if I didn't tell him where she was. We need to hide her, Keith. I thought she would be safe here. I was wrong. Jack is getting worse. I used to talk to him and get him to calm down. He's full of rage, like your father was at the end."

In all the years I've known her, I've never seen Fiona cry. Ever. I gently guide her up from the chair and sit her on the bed.

"You need to find Victoria and protect her and that baby," she pleads.

"But…" I start to protest.

"But nothing. Victoria is his target. Jack's never been a good sport when losing. He likes to be in control."

My phone says I have a missed call and a text message from Gemma. I read the message.

"Gemma tried to warn me about Jack being here. She must have seen his car."

"Do you think Victoria's with her?" Fiona asks me.

I type out a text to Gemma: *Where are you? Are you with Victoria?*

She replies instantly. *Yes. We're at your house.*

I told her to lock the doors and that I'm on my way. I leave my truck at Fiona's as a precaution.

"Don't worry. They're safe. But I'm not leaving you here. You're coming with me," I tell Fiona.

For the first time in a long time, Fiona doesn't argue. She takes a minute to put herself back together and grabs her purse.

"Let's go," she says. The determination on her face is the Fiona I know.

***

"Gemma? Gemma?" I call out as I shut the door behind Fiona and me. "It's me."

I hear footsteps pad down the stairs, and Gemma runs to me. She's shaking. I hold her and kiss the top of her head.

"Are you okay?" I ask. "Where are Victoria and the baby?"

"They're upstairs resting. I hope that's okay."

"Of course it is. Did he see them?"

"I don't think so. We left my house, and we didn't see the car until we were at your doorstep. We were here, inside, when he drove off. Keith, why would Victoria's husband be at Fiona's?"

I turn to Fiona. "You'd better explain to them. You three should stay here, though. I'm finding that son-of-a-bitch."

"Here, bring Chester with you," Gemma says. "He'll follow your lead."

"You don't know what this guy is capable of," I tell her. "I don't want Chester getting hurt."

"But you *do* know what Chester is capable of. You have his commands. Use them," she says. "He'll listen to you."

As if on cue, Chester walks over to me and heels.

"Well, okay, then. I guess it's you and me, bud," I tell him. He gives me his paw and then stands at attention.

Victoria slowly climbs down the stairs. "What's happening?" she asks. Gemma explains, and Victoria says, "Wait, I saw on TV that dogs need something that smells like the person to track them. Is that true?"

I nod. "You have an object that belongs to him? A T-shirt or memento you brought with you?" I ask her.

A look of defeat appears on her face as she realizes that whatever she may have had of Jack's had burned in the fire.

"I do," Fiona says. "After he tied me up, he wiped his face with a towel. It should still be on the bed where he threw it."

Fiona hands me her house key, and Chester and I are on our way. We swiftly make our way to Fiona's, grab the towel, and get into my truck. Chester sniffs at the towel as we drive.

"You got it, bud? That's who we want, okay?" I say. Chester gives me a single, deep bark in affirmation.

"Let's go find my evil brother," I tell him.

***

Chester and I drive to the end of Laurelville. The town is laid out in a grid pattern, so we take our time as we move from one neighborhood to the next, to the businesses, and to the parks.

After hours of searching for Jack and his blue car, we headed back to my truck. Has he left town without getting what he wants? That's not like my brother at all.

Chester and I pull back onto Sycamore and into my driveway. Fiona, Gemma, and Victoria have made a feast in my kitchen. As Chester and I entered the house, all kinds of wonderful scents hit our noses. Chester barks and runs over to Gemma.

"Hey, baby, did you do some hard work today?" Gemma asks him, then gives him a good scratch under his neck. Then to me, "Did you find him?"

"He sure did. He must be exhausted from all that sniffing," I tell her. She comes over and kisses me. "And no. No sign of Jack."

"You must be tired, too," she tells me.

"I think frustrated is more the word," I say. "I really thought we would find him."

# Chapter 50



While Keith is out looking for Jack, Gemma and Fiona keep busy cooking. It's a good way to keep everyone distracted from what happened today. Gemma acts nervously around Fiona, but I'm not sure why. Then I remember. The gun. Once the dishes are baking, boiling, and simmering, Fiona walks over to Keith's wine rack and opens a bottle of wine.

"Umm, are you sure Keith is okay with us drinking his wine?" Gemma asks. "That's a 2016 BV de Latour."

Fiona's smile reaches her eyes, and I think she's about to laugh. Instead, she uncorks the wine, grabs three glasses from the cupboard, and pats the back of two kitchen chairs. "Sit down, ladies. I think there's something we need to discuss. But first, liquid courage."

She holds up the bottle of Cabernet and pours us each a glass. I slide mine over to Gemma. In one swoop, Fiona swallows hers.

Gemma and I look at each other. Why would Fiona need liquid courage? I'm afraid to find out.

Fiona explains how she helped Tony get the fake IDs for both of us. She carefully devised a plan for us to be on the move for two months. I chuckle and realize I had been duped. Tony had taken all the credit for how smoothly our move to Laurelville had been. Fiona was the puppet master all this time. From the house to the baby's room to my new job, Fiona had it all mapped out. *But why?*

"I appreciate everything you've done for us, Fiona. But I don't understand why," I tell her.

Fiona looks over at Sebastian, who is now awake and smiling.

"Because that little boy you have right there is my grandson," she says, and I can tell by the tear in her eye that everything she has done has come from a place of love.

"You mean Jack is your son? But he told me his mother died."

"She did. I'm his stepmother. I raised him. And his brother. I have a biological son as well, but he was raised by his aunt."

"He has a brother?" Gemma says, confused.

"Keith," Fiona says.

"Wait a minute. Tony was raised by his aunt. In Italy," I say, putting the pieces of the puzzle together.

I look at Gemma, and she looks at me. She takes her glass, refills it, and gulps it down.

"So, you're Jack and Keith's stepmother? Why did Jack never mention you?" I ask her.

"And why didn't Keith?" Gemma adds.

"And why didn't Tony ever mention that Jack was raised by his own mother? That would make them stepbrothers."

"Ladies, I think you understand the big picture now. The why isn't important, and it's a story for another day. What's important now is that we keep you and Sebastian safe, Victoria. We don't know where Jack is, but your best friend is dead. We can't have more mess-ups."

***

Sebastian sleeps soundly in his front pack. Keith escorts Gemma, Chester, and me back to her place. He makes sure all the windows and doors are locked and secure before he heads back home. Exhausted, I plop down on the couch as gently as I can. I have two big wet spots on my boobs from breastmilk, but I'm too tired to care. Sebastian stirs as I take him out of the pack and swaddle him in a blanket to place him in his bassinet. I go about my business of personal care, which includes changing my maxi pad to pumping two bags of breast milk.

When I'm done, Gemma comes out of her bedroom, her hair wet from the shower.

"If you want to shower, I'll keep an ear out for Sebastian," she tells me.

I gladly take her advice. The warm water feels amazing on my body. I feel achy from all the stress and giving birth this week. As I get out of the shower, I listen for Sebastian's cries, but it's quiet. He must still be asleep. I can't hear Gemma either.

Usually, she's in the kitchen clattering pots and pans. But it also occurs to me that maybe she's at her table working. I slather on some body butter and wrap a towel around myself. I assess how I'm feeling. I poke at my belly, which is now mostly loose skin. My muscles are achy. Back home, I used to work out and do yoga several times a week. The pregnancy, along with my lack of activity, must be what is causing the body aches. I towel-dry my hair and sit down on my bed. I peer into the bassinet to check on Sebastian. I do a double-take. It's empty. Panic sets in, and I rush out to the living room.

"Are you okay?" Gemma asks.

There on the couch is Gemma, bundling a very happy Sebastian on her lap. A baby bottle sits on the coffee table along with two glasses of wine and a simple spread of cheese and crackers. I must have looked like a crazy woman rushing out like that.

"Sorry, I guess I'm still on edge," I tell her, taking a deep breath.

"Sebastian woke up while you were in the shower, so I made him a bottle. He wasn't hungry, though. I think he wants to play," she laughs, as she wiggles the finger he has clamped his little fist to. He coos loudly, and I laugh. He has excellent hand-eye coordination, like his daddy.

I go back into the bedroom to throw on a T-shirt and shorts. When I come back out, Sebastian is happily sucking on his bottle. His little hands wrapped around it, as if to say, "Don't go anywhere. I'm not done."

"Hungry guy," Gemma says.

"He's a good baby. Eat, burp, poop, sleep. Easy," I tell her. "I'm glad I pumped earlier. Mama needs a little relaxation today. I'll pump and dump later since I don't think Sebastian will like milk a la pinot noir. I don't know about other moms, but I feel like all I've been doing is pumping. Is that normal for my milk to come in this quickly this early?"

Gemma laughs. "You're asking the wrong person. Do you want me to ask Ali?"

Now it's my turn to laugh. I shake my head. "No, it's fine."

I take a sip of wine and savor the velvety texture in my mouth. "This tastes amazing."

"Not as good as the Latour, but I can't imagine not having any wine for what, nine, ten months?"

I nod. "Yeah, closer to ten months. I stopped as soon as I found out I was pregnant."

"So, what's he like?" Gemma asks me.

"What's who like?"

"Sebastian's daddy."

"Well..." I start. And then I tell her the full story about how I met Jack. And his friend, Tony.

# Chapter 51

KEITH

"We need to figure this out, Fiona. Innocent people will get hurt. We need to find Jack before he finds us."

"I didn't think he'd ever be back here," Fiona says. "He disowned all of us after your father died."

"But you knew there was a chance," I tell her.

It's true. After our father died, Jack went off the rails. He was a lot like our dad; very intelligent and oozing with charisma, but then a switch would flip, and this angry, violent person would materialize. After our dad retired from the National Guard, we thought he and Fiona would live a comfortable life in Carlsbad. I received a phone call from my dad one day. He announced that he and Fiona were moving to a little town south of San Diego. Unbeknownst to us, there would be bad days ahead. Moving was Fiona's way of trying to solve the problem. By the time we found out, it was too late.

"I never meant to kill him, Keith. You know that," Fiona says. "It was self-defense. Jack was there for God's sake."

"We all know that. No one realized how bad things were between you and Dad until that day. By the time Dad retired, Jack and I were out of the house. Jack isn't telling the cops. Not all these years later. He was an accomplice."

***

It was Thanksgiving Day. Fiona and my dad had recently moved into the house on Sycamore Way. Fiona thought that living in a small town where the culture was slower and calmer would put a damper on my father's violent outbursts. Fiona, being the badass realtor she is, could get a deal on four houses on the same street. Hers and my dad's, the one Victoria and Emilio were staying in, Brooks and Ali's house, and the house I'm in.

I arrived at the house before Jack, and my father seemed to be in good spirits. I could tell Fiona was walking on eggshells, though, so I did my best to help her around the kitchen and with the table setting.

"So, Keith, now that you're finished with your commitment to the Army, what are you planning on doing with yourself?" my father asked.

To some, this would seem like an innocent question a father would ask a son. In our family, the question was a fully loaded AK47.

"I interviewed with several companies and took a position with a top construction firm in Sacramento," I told him, showing no weakness in my answer. If there's anything my dad hated, it was weakness.

"I see. What does it pay?"

And another loaded question. If the salary was too low, according to my dad's standards, I would get berated for not knowing my worth. If I gave my dad an inflated number, he would ask me who I thought I was to deserve that type of money. It was a losing situation, but I was experienced in playing this game.

"Low six figures," I said.

"Hmph," my dad answered.

Fiona brought a bottle of his favorite whiskey to the table. The whiskey was a version of Russian roulette in our family. We were either safe, or we weren't.

A loud knock at the door sounded, and Fiona almost spilled the whiskey. She covered her mouth with her other hand to stifle a nervous laugh while I got up to answer the door.

"Brother!" Jack said. He shook my hand and then pulled me in close for a hug. I slapped him on the back, and we turned to head back into the kitchen.

"Hi, Mama," he said, hugging Fiona. "Hey, Pops."

"Jack," my dad said.

Fiona served dinner, and we ate quietly, not saying a word, although I gave Fiona a nod and a smile to thank her for the delicious meal. My dad was on his sixth or seventh whiskey by the time we finished dinner. He was about to fall asleep in his chair, a good sign.

"Marcel?" Fiona said in a soft, gentle tone. "Why don't you go make yourself comfortable in the living room while the boys and I clean up?"

My dad's eyes opened to reveal bloodshot whites, his face washed over in crimson. His voice boomed, ricocheting off the walls.

"Goddammit, Fiona. If I want to take a nap at my own god-damn dinner table, then that's what I'll do."

Fiona, Jack, and I freeze.

"I'm sorry, Dear. You're right," Fiona said, the fear seeping into her eyes.

My father stood up and charged at her like a bull in a bullring. His hands outstretched as he lunged for her throat. Fiona was quick and dodged my drunk father's advances. She moved to the left. He was so drunk he stumbled. But then, he grabbed onto the counter to get his bearings. Fiona grabbed an empty cast-iron pan from the stovetop and held it out like a shield to stop his advances. My father's nose came barreling into the solid piece of iron. He knocked her to the ground and stumbled into the table. A plate and a steak knife fell onto the floor, and he went down with them. He crushed Fiona as he threw a fit of blind rage-filled punches, the cast-iron pan sandwiched between them. Fiona shielded her face with her hands as Jack and I reached for his legs to pull him off her. Our father was a large man and weighed approximately two hundred and seventy pounds, so it was not an easy feat. He grabbed her skirt, pulling it with him. Fiona flipped over, army-crawling away from danger. My dad broke loose and tackled her once more. Jack and I were on top of them at one point, and what I remember next is a bit blurry. Fiona somehow reached the steak knife that had fallen on the floor. She plunged it into the side of my father's neck repeatedly until Jack and I could pull him off Fiona. My father flailed wildly and grasped at his neck. There was blood everywhere. The kitchen looked like a scene from an 80s horror movie.

"In hindsight, it was so stupid of me not to burn the body. What was I thinking, having you and Jack bury the body at the 251 house?"

"Stop blaming yourself. Dad wasn't in his right mind. He would have killed you if you didn't kill him first. Jack and I could barely get him off you."

Fiona and I sit quietly. We recalled everything our family had gone through. Setting fire to her own house had been the last resort to protect us all and keep the family secret buried. And now with Jack, it's like history has come back to bite us in the ass full circle. It's up to us to break the cycle.

"We should probably get Tony over here. He's as much a part of this as we all are," Fiona says, picking up her phone.

# Chapter 52



Gemma calls the next day and asks if I'd like to grab some lunch with her. Although I'd love to spend every waking hour with Gemma, I'm behind on the work for Fiona's deck and want to get it finished before the rainy season commences. Plus, I need to stick around here to keep an eye out for my brother. I tell Gemma I need to take a raincheck on lunch, but ask her if she would like to go out to dinner later that evening. She perks up at the sound of this.

"I'd love to take you somewhere fancy—on a proper date," I tell her. "I heard Landry's Seafood in Locke City is spectacular."

"I love Landry's!" she exclaims, and I can picture her grin from ear to ear. "My dad used to bring us there for special occasions. But what about Victoria? Maybe we shouldn't be so far away from her."

I think for a minute. She has a good point.

"I know," she says, and I can feel her smile radiating through the phone. "Darby wants to do a healing session for Victoria. I'll call her and see if Victoria can hang out with her tonight. Seamus will be home, so they'll be safe, and he won't bother them if they're in a session."

"It's a date then. Pick you up at around 6:00 p.m.?"

"That sounds perfect. I'll see you later," she says.

My phone rings a few minutes later. It's Fiona telling me to pick Tony up from Gator's house. She wants to go over the plan to find Jack. I can tell from the sound of her voice that she means business. No one threatens Fiona and gets away with it.

# Chapter 53

Victoria

"Are you sure you'll be okay here by yourself?" Gemma asks me.

"I'm not by myself. I have Sebastian and Chester here to keep me company. Plus, you'll be gone, what? An hour at the most?"

"Not even an hour. I need to pick up food for Chester and buy a few items I forgot for the potluck this weekend. I'll put Chester in the backyard for a bit. You can let him back in if he comes to the patio door."

Chester looks up at Gemma and whines. I laugh.

"I know. I know. Okay. See you in a bit," Gemma says and leads Chester out back.

After Gemma leaves, I double-check that the doors and windows are secure. You can never be too safe. Sebastian snoozes next to me, his little arms in the air, and I flip through the latest issue of Vogue. My phone pings with a text from Ali to me and

Gemma and me. Hey, ladies! Are you home? I'm headed out and wanted to drop off Gemma's dish from the other night.

I answer: Gemma is running errands, but I'm here. Stop by anytime.

The three dots appear followed by: See you soon!

Thirty seconds later, a loud knock pounds on the front door, which makes me jump. Why in the world would Ali knock so loud? I glance over at Sebastian, who is still asleep.

I open the door to greet Ali, leading with, "That's a strong…" I trail off, only to be met with a gaze I know all too well. It's Jack.

***

My first instinct is to shut the door. But Jack is too quick. He's holding a pistol and has it pointed at me. He shoves his leg forward and wedges his foot in the door. *Shit. What do I do? He's much stronger than I am.* My only option is to run and find something to protect myself and Sebastian.

"What do you want, Jack?" I ask him. I backpedal as he slams the door behind him.

My focus is on what I can grab to defend myself.

"I want my wife to come back home," he says. "You said you loved me."

"I…I can't, Jack. We can't be together anymore. Please leave me alone."

"You're my wife. Of course you can. You belong to me. You told me you loved me."

Secretly, I'm hoping that someone will see his car in front of the house. Gemma and I told Ali and everyone else on the block to be on the lookout for Jack's blue car. Ali should be here soon.

"You need to leave, Jack. My neighbor will be here soon, and she'll see your car. She'll call the cops." Even as I hear myself saying this, I know it'll never work. Jack isn't fooled easily.

"Your neighbor?" he laughs. "You mean Fiona? She's at work. She won't save you. Plus, I walked here. I couldn't risk anyone seeing me."

He laughs again, but is interrupted by a knock at the door. *Oh my god. It's Ali. This is my chance.* Jack grabs me and jabs the gun into my side.

"Fucking nosy ass neighbors. I never did like this street. Everyone is in everybody's business. I guess that's what happens when your mother buys the neighborhood."

Jack swings the door open. It's Ali. Gemma's dish falls to the ground with a loud shatter as her eyes meet Jack's. They exchange a look that is a mix of fear and anger. Ali belts out a blood-curdling scream and takes a step back. Before she can run, Jack reaches for her and catches the back of her shirt. She struggles to pull away from him, but he pulls her so hard into him that she trips on the doorstep and falls. He points the gun at her. Like me, she has no choice but to do what he says. We are both his prisoners.

"Get up. Get in here," Jack says, his green eyes flaming with anger. "Well, well, isn't this a treat."

"Johnny..." she says, and suddenly I realize. Johnny is Jack. Jack is Johnny. The boyfriend Gemma told me Ali killed. That scar on Jack's chest. It wasn't from a car accident. It was from Ali.

"Hello, Margot."

"But...but...you're supposed to be dead."

"Surprise!"

# Chapter 54

KEITH

"How'd you learn how to do this?" Tony asks as he takes in the beautiful landscaping. The deck's last coat of varnish is drying as we enjoy a cold beer. I show him some of the newly planted flowers that border the yard—gardenias, marigolds, verbena, and Fiona's favorite, lavender.

"Experience mostly. Years of working for other people. I picked up on skills here and there," I tell him. "I always said I would go back to trade school and become an electrician, but it never seemed like the right time."

Tony and I are six years apart. He's barely thirty. Jack is thirty-four, and I'm thirty-six. Fiona gave birth to Tony at the beginning of her career as a real estate agent in Carlsbad. Fiona never told Jack or me about Tony. We figured we were the only sons Fiona ever had. Heck, I didn't even know she was married before she met my dad. When Fiona asked me to do her a favor and move to Laurelville for a few months, she told me about the son she never talked about. I was shocked that Fiona never told us about Tony, but she had her reasons. Fiona had paid for Tony's move to the Bay Area to help her keep tabs on Jack. I guess Fiona had a sixth sense that Jack would be back to his old abusive self after he almost killed two of his ex-girlfriends.

"I'm getting hungry. I've got some sandwich stuff in the fridge."

"I'm hungry, too," Tony says, and we walk around to the side door to avoid stepping on the deck.

A piercing scream penetrates the air, and a rush of adrenaline surges through my body. I bolt into the house, Tony on my tail, and grab my gun, keys, and phone. He pulls a large butcher knife from the block on the counter, and we sprint out the front door.

"Where?" Tony and I stand in the middle of the street, praying for any clue as to where the scream came from. That's when I see Freddy run out of his house. He points us toward Gemma's house. We make our way three houses down. Gemma must still be out because her car isn't parked in the driveway. That means Victoria is home alone. Tony follows me around the backside of Gemma's house. We stop before we reach the back sliding glass door, the one I have the key to. Chester is pressed up against Gemma's back door, growling.

"Chester," I whisper. "Komm!"

Chester obediently runs over to me and sits at my feet. "Blieb," I tell him, giving him the command to "stay." I don't want Chester getting hurt in all of this. It would kill Gemma if something happened to him. Chester looks up at Tony in recognition.

"Hey, boy," Tony says, and Chester gives him a paw to shake. I guess Chester has spent enough time with Emilio and Victoria to know who Tony is. I tell Tony to stay there with Chester while I sneak up to see what's happening. I keep my body as close to the house as possible and listen in. The baby is screaming, and then I hear Victoria, "Please. Please give him to me. Jack, please."

The latch on the back door is locked. I take a chance and peek in. Victoria and Ali are on the couch, trembling. Jack has Sebastian, who is wailing. *Shit. He found Ali, too?*

Victoria reaches for Sebastian and continues to plead for Jack to give him to her.

"So, this is what I lost my wife to? This shitty little screaming thing?" Jack yells. He thrusts the baby at Victoria. "Shut him up and put him in the other room. I'm sick of it."

Victoria cradles Sebastian, trying to calm him as she walks him into the bedroom. Jack keeps his eyes on her as he waves the gun in Ali's face. Ali's hands are up as she pleads with him not to do anything stupid.

"So, this is where you've been all these years," Jack says. "After you tried to kill me. You thought I was dead, didn't you?"

Ali gives a slight nod.

"Well, I'm not," Jack grins and gets up closer to Ali. He touches his forehead to hers and shoves the gun underneath her chin. "I'm right here, Margot. I should pull this and put you out of your misery, you dumb fucking bitch. I taught you everything. Gave you everything."

Victoria comes back into the room without Sebastian, and Jack shoves her back onto the couch.

"Where is it?" Jack asks Victoria.

"Where's what?"

"Don't play stupid. Where's the money?"

"Jack, what are you talking about?"

Jack shoves the gun into Victoria's mouth, and she whimpers. The tears pour down her face.

"Do I really need to spell it out for you? The money that you inherited from your grandparents. The quarter of a million dollars. Scarlett told me about it. You were holding out on me!"

Victoria shakes her head, and Jack pulls the gun back.

"I don't have it."

"Bullshit. Scarlett said you were allowed to access it when you turned thirty. I searched the house next door, and it wasn't there. Where is the money?"

Victoria takes a deep breath and then glares at Jack.

"I rolled it into a trust for Sebastian. All of it. I'm the only one who can access it."

Jack hits Victoria with the butt of the gun, and she falls sideways onto the couch. He paces back and forth.

"You know what? This is such a surprise. It's like two-in-one! I have both my girlfriend and my wife back. I think we should celebrate, don't you? The only one who's missing is Sasha. That hippie dippy bitch better not be living on this street too," he says as an evil laugh escaped from the depths of his belly.

I swallow hard at his comment. If he only knew our mother had been keeping every woman he abused under her mother bird wings, he'd have a shit fit. I pray Darby doesn't find her way over.

Jack heads into the kitchen and finds a bottle of Prosecco in the fridge. As he goes through the cupboards for a glass, Ali tries to help Victoria up. I wave at her through the back door and put my finger up to my lips. Ali nods. I need to act quickly before Jack does something he regrets. He walks back into the room with a glass of Prosecco and holds it up.

"Here's to us. And who do I have to thank for this? My dear, dear mother. Cheers to Fiona for reuniting our family."

***

While Jack continues to rant, I move back next to Tony and Chester. We round the corner to the side of the house, and I pull my phone out to notify Fiona to call the police. Within five minutes, we see three police vehicles pull up in front of Gemma's. No lights, no sirens. Smart, Fiona. The only question is: how will we get everyone out alive? Jack won't give up without a fight. I peek around the corner and walk back to the door. He's still ranting.

"Let's play a game. You both like games, don't you? I trained both of you well. Eeny meeny miny moe," Jack sings as he points the gun at one woman after another. "Catch a tiger by the, muther fuckin' toe."

Without warning, he fires a bullet into Ali's stomach. Anger makes my face turn red hot. She keels over in pain, and an almost soundless scream escapes her lips as she grabs at her midsection and slides down off the couch. Jack laughs maniacally. Victoria reaches down to help her, but Jack is quick.

"Nope, nope. You stay there," he says, pointing back to the couch. "Aww, did that hurt? Did Margot get what she deserved?"

He turns to Victoria and says, "Maybe you and I should take a trip to the bank. What do you think, Cara? I know I could use a quarter of a million dollars for a lot of things. That baby in there doesn't need money."

Victoria stays silent as Ali curls up in the fetal position. I step back and whisper to Tony, "The police are here. We've got to be ready for this."

"I'll sneak out front to tell the police what's happening," Tony says.

"Go," I tell him. "Hide the knife."

As Tony runs out front, I gesture for Chester to follow me, which he does obediently. Jack pulls Victoria off the couch, his arm around her neck, the gun in the small of her back. This is it. The question is, will he take her out the front or the back door? The echo of a police radio breaks the silence.

"Shit," I whisper to myself. *So much for the police being stealthy.*

"Who the fuck called the cops?" Jack yells. Both women are silent. The tears run down their faces. Jack and Victoria approach the back door. She pleads for her life as he commands her to open the door. Chester and I move back to allow some space between us and the door. I take aim and release the safety, ready to shoot if I need to. Chester and I exchange glances.

"Please, you don't need to do this. I'll do what you say. I'll come back home to you. You can have the money," Victoria sobs.

"Too late. We're gonna have a little fun, though. Think of it as a last hurrah. You know, that really was selfish of you and Tony to run off together. My friend. Where the hell is he, by the way?"

Victoria steps across the threshold. Her eyes find me instantly. For a split second, I think she might scream, but her mouth only falls open, shock freezing her in place. I tilt my head to signal for her to move to her left on my command. With her head facing forward, eyes on me, she tips her chin in acknowledgment. Jack is close behind her, his gun in the small of her back. My heart lurches. There's no time to think. Only to act.

"Fass!" I command Chester, my gun aimed at Jack's torso. Victoria lunges to the left. She falls to the ground and bear-crawls across the lawn. With lightning-fast speed, Chester lunges forward and attacks Jack at the thigh, his growl loud and vicious. I fire multiple shots, the sound ricocheting in the air as the bullets penetrate my brother's midsection one after the other. Jack crumbles into a heap. I run over and call Chester off Jack, who is now lying still on the ground.

*He's still my little brother,* I remind myself, the weapon still warm in his grip. I kick his gun away. *But I can't let him win. Not this time.*

Suddenly, the house is full of shouting voices. Police swarm in, followed by paramedics. They ordered me to put my gun down and stand back. Jack is barely breathing, and paramedics load him onto a stretcher. My breath heaves in ragged gulps, and for the first time, I see my hands trembling. The paramedics stabilize Ali and get her onto a stretcher as well.

Tony runs to Cara, who is underneath Gemma's picnic table. She's curled tight.

"It's okay, it's okay," Tony whispers, though the words sound broken. As he rolls Cara over, Tony cradles her neck. Cara's eyelids flutter rapidly as Tony places a gentle kiss on her forehead. I hold my breath, all the muscles in my chest tight as wire. Cara's body stops shaking, and Tony's expression changes as he notices his hand is covered in blood.

"No! No!" Tony yells and immediately puts pressure on Cara's wound. Paramedics rush over to help, picking her up and placing her on a stretcher. That's when I see it. The large red bloom on her back. The sound of the ricochet when I shot Jack was that of him pulling the trigger simultaneously, the bullet striking Cara in the back. When Tony's eyes finally meet mine, it's enough to tear me apart. *No. God, no. Please let Cara be okay. Please don't tell me this was all for nothing.*

Chester, who is by my side, lets out a quiet whimper, his muzzle caked with blood. I kneel and give him a good scratch behind both ears. He's panting heavily.

"You did so good, buddy. Good boy, Chester. Let's go find Mom."

Chester follows me out front, where Gemma and Fiona stand on the sidewalk in front of Fiona's house. They both have tears in their eyes. Fiona grabs my arm.

"What happened?"

I don't know where to start. Everything is one gigantic clusterfuck.

# Chapter 55



FIVE YEARS LATER

Ali

As I cut up the fruit for the children, Brooks comes from behind me and kisses me on the neck. I giggle, and he squeezes me tighter and says, "I love you so much."

"I love you so much, too," I tell him.

"I don't know what I would ever do without you," he says. "I still think back to the day I thought I was going to lose you. I never want to experience that again."

I smile at him. Brooks is a good man. I knew this from the moment I met him. That's why I chose him to be the father of my child. Intelligent, secure, strong, generous, and wealthy. What more did a girl need? I rub my belly and wonder what this little one will look like. Will he be like Sydney, precocious and intuitive? I guess we'll find out in three months.

"How's my baby?" Brooks asks.

"Active. I don't remember Sydney moving around this much, so maybe it's a boy thing. I remember Victoria telling me that Sebastian was a kicker and a mover."

Brooks laughs. We both turn to hear the echo of little voices coming from the backyard. Two sets of small feet noisily slap the hardwood floor.

"Mom, Seabass says that he'll grow up to be taller than me," Sydney says, a pout forming at the corners of her mouth. "I told him he can't be because I'm a lot older."

Sebastian climbs up onto the barstool next to Sydney and says, "I'm going to grow bigger, though. Because boys grow bigger than girls."

"Sometimes, Buddy. But not always," Brooks says, ruffling Sebastian's hair. "I guess we'll have to wait and see. But no matter who's bigger, Mom and I will always love both of you."

This makes Sydney and Sebastian smile, and a little dimple appears in each of their left cheeks. The gift Johnny, or Jack, gave them both. That and their green eyes. Deep down, I hope those are the only things they've inherited from him.

Fiona and Tony stop by all the time to visit. I guess Fiona knew all along that Sydney was Johnny's child, but we've made a pact not to tell Brooks. It would break his heart if he knew she wasn't biologically his. I still can't believe I didn't recognize Keith. I guess back when I was Margot, all I could do was think about how to survive.

# Chapter 56



I should probably write a book about all the bullshit that has happened to me in the forty-one years I've been on this earth. Gemma tells me it's a good idea and that I would find it therapeutic. I don't know, though. She doesn't even know the half of it.

"Hey, Babe," she says, coming down the stairs.

I hand her a cup of coffee and a warm scone. She takes a bite.

"Mm, whoever made these scones should get an award," she says. "Delicious."

I laugh, then wrap my hands around her belly.

"How are my girls?" I ask.

Her cheeks flush. "This one is giving mama a little heartburn, but other than that, we're doing well."

Gemma and I had a small wedding ceremony in the park two years ago. Chester was the ring bearer, and almost the whole town came to celebrate our nuptials. Gemma was the most beautiful bride I had ever seen. Ali and Fiona arranged the reception and did an amazing job of it all.

"I can't believe Ali and I are due at the exact same time. It'll be so fun raising the little ones together," Gemma says.

Gemma is glowing from the pregnancy. Her hair was thicker and shinier than before. I bend down to give her a long, passionate kiss that lingers until she pulls away. She covers her mouth as a little burp escapes.

"Sorry," she says. "I guess your daughter doesn't like us kissing."

# Chapter 57

Victoria

Dear Sebastian,

If you're reading this letter, it means I couldn't stay as long as I wanted to. I know that the neighbors on Sycamore Way will take good care of you, though. Sydney always wanted a baby brother.

Even before you were born, I knew you were special. The little flutters in my belly when you wanted to say hello made me smile and brightened each day. You made me brave in ways I didn't know I could be.

I wish I could be there to experience all your firsts, but it wasn't in the stars. I hope you grow up to be strong and kind. Treat others how you would want to be treated. I hope you feel love and happiness every day of your life. There may be days when you feel lost or sad. Please don't ever feel that you're alone. Your aunties—Gemma, Ali, Darby, and Penelope—will keep you safe. Fiona is like the mother I never had, and I truly believe she will treat you like the grandson she never had.

When I met your dad, my future was the brightest it had ever been. Sadly, I was mistaken. There are so many milestones I wish I could be there for. I wish I could have gotten to know you, and you me. But since I'm not here with you, here's a little bit about me, your mama.

I was born Cara Ann Maxwell on May 10th, 1988. I was raised by my grandparents and stayed with a friend named Scarlett growing up. Sadly, Scarlett passed away right before I wrote this letter. Your father, Jack, was in the Army. As far as I know, he doesn't have any living relatives. Our relationship was abusive. I ran away from him to save us both from his wrath, but if you're reading this, there's a chance that he's either deceased or incarcerated. I was a nurse back home in the Bay Area, and I loved my job. I loved helping people and caring for them. Some of my favorite foods are peanut butter, gummy bears, and street tacos. When I was pregnant with you, I craved beef jerky. I can tie a cherry stem with my tongue. I can also roll my tongue, a trait that is usually passed down, so give it a try.

I moved to Sycamore Way with your dad's friend, Tony. Our fake names were Victoria and Emilio. Tony saved our lives, but disappeared before he could meet you. Should he ever reappear, please tell him I love him and owe him everything.

Most of all, what you should know about me is that I loved you with every bit of my heart. Although I am not there to hold you, please know that I am still with you—in your heart, in your soul, and in every breath you take. You will always be my greatest accomplishment, and my love will live on through you, my sweet boy.

I love you to pieces.

Mom

# Chapter 58

Darby

My daughter sits on the living room floor, putting together a diorama for her third-grade class. Pieces of construction paper, moss, tree bark, and tiny pebbles litter the ground, and I sit down next to her to assist.

"Wow, Mona, that's amazing," I tell her. "I love the little bridge with the lanterns."

"Thanks, Mom. Sydney helped me with it. But she had to go home and do her own homework."

I nod. "Well, you both did an excellent job. Your teacher will love it."

Ramona gives me a wide smile, her green eyes shiny, and her dimple deep.

It's been nine years since I could escape the wrath of Jack. I never told the ladies of Sycamore about my past troubles. I couldn't risk Seamus finding out that Ramona wasn't his. The ladies think I dote too much on my husband. If they only knew. Seamus is my saving grace. After hearing about Ali and Victoria, I've come to understand Fiona a bit more as well. More often than not, I can read another person's energy quickly. I know if they have good or bad energy, as well as if they're sneaky. There are only two people who I could never read. Jack and Fiona. Now I know why.

The others don't know that Ramona is Sydney and Sebastian's half-sibling. It's a secret I'm not willing to tell. I know Keith and Fiona will keep it that way. Their protection is what has kept my family alive.

# Chapter 60



The morning light drifts across Sycamore Way. It paints the street in soft gold. The neighborhood, with all its secrets and fractures, is strangely still, as if exhaling after holding its breath for far too long.

Not everyone survived to see this calm. Jack's death lingers in the air like a stain that refused to wash out. His rage, his control, his violence—all of it had culminated in an end as brutal as his life had been. The story of how he died had already warped into rumor, carried in hushed conversations over fences and at the grocery store. But the people who truly knew the truth carried it differently, like an ache deep in their bones.

Some had vanished into silence, while others carried scars that would never fully heal. But the living had made choices that stitched together the fragile fabric of survival.

Tony moves through the neighborhood like a ghost, fixing cars, nodding to neighbors, but never letting anyone close enough to see the truth. At night, when the street is quiet, he sometimes replays every moment with Cara in his mind. The stolen glances, the unspoken words, the near-confessions he never had the courage to give voice to. He tells himself he protected her in his own way, but the ache of it not having been enough gnawed at him endlessly.

Across the street, Ali steps outside and waves at Gemma as if the dark undercurrents of the past years had never existed. That was the neighborhood's trick. Smiles and small talk over fences, casseroles at the door, laughter carried by summer picnics. Yet beneath it all lay shared knowledge that no one dared voice aloud. They had all seen too much. They all knew too much.

Victoria's name is rarely spoken now, and when it is, it comes with careful pauses, as though invoking a ghost. She left behind more than just a house filled with echoes. She left questions, regrets, and the kind of secrets that spread through whispers long after the door slammed shut.

The wind carries the scent of fresh-cut grass. The children's laughter spills into the street. Life, relentless and ordinary, marched forward. Sycamore Way would keep its secrets. And those who remained would keep smiling, keep surviving, and keep pretending that everything was fine.

Because in Laurelville, survival isn't about forgetting. It is about learning to live with what you cannot forget.

The End

# *Acknowledgements*

Where do I even start? Deciding to write a standalone thriller really kicked me out of my comfort zone. To top it off, I decided to make it a huge challenge for both myself and my editors, Laura and RB, by writing the whole book in first person, present-tense. So sorry guys. What was I thinking? Thank you for sticking with me through this. You're truly the best and have taught me things I never knew existed. English is quite a tricky language.

Writing is such an enjoyable experience for me—a getaway from the stresses of daily life. I love creating characters and giving them personalities and identities. I could not have done it without the patience of my other half, Rich. Thank you for sticking by my side through everything. I love you.

I'd also like to thank my beta readers, Stephen, Allana, and Rebecca. Your feedback help to shape this story, and to make it better for all of my readers. I appreciate you so much.

And to my friend and personal training client, Andrea. Brainstorming ideas with you is always so fun. I hope the real Keith likes his character.

# About the author

**ABOUT THE AUTHOR**

Kristina Fox is a certified personal trainer based in the San Francisco Bay Area, where she combines her passion for wellness with a lifelong love of storytelling. A dedicated reader since the age of three, she brings her deep appreciation for mystery and suspense to her writing. Kristina's favorite pastimes include sipping wine, enjoying sushi, and competing in lively board games—all preferably in the company of family. Mysteries remain her favorite escape.

**Also by Kristina Fox**

The Kelsey James Fitness Mystery Series

Candy & Cardio-novella

Time Under Tension

Double Progression

Maximum Limit

**Thrillers**

**Silent Harvest-novella**

The Neighborhood Knows

# Thank you!

Thank you so much for reading What the Neighborhood Knows. If you liked this book, please consider checking out my other books.

Please consider leaving a review on Amazon and/or Goodreads. I would greatly appreciate it. Be sure to subscribe to my email newsletter for free books, book launch updates and announcements, and live events. Visit kristinafox.com for more details.